The Buffalo Knife

BOOKS BY WILLIAM O. STEELE

The Buffalo Knife

Flaming Arrows

The Perilous Road

Winter Danger

The Buffalo Knife

William O. Steele

WITH AN INTRODUCTION BY JEAN FRITZ

AN ODYSSEY / HARCOURT YOUNG CLASSIC

HARCOURT, INC.

Orlando   Austin   New York   San Diego   Toronto   London

www.HarcourtBooks.com

First Harcourt Young Classics edition 2004
First Odyssey Classics edition 1990
First published 1952

Library of Congress Cataloging-in-Publication Data
Steele, William O., 1917–
The buffalo knife/William O. Steele; with an introduction by Jean Fritz.
p.   cm.
"An Odyssey/Harcourt Young Classic."
Summary: In 1782, nine-year-old Andy, his family, and
neighbors make a dangerous journey by flatboat down a thousand
miles of the Tennessee River to make a new home.
[1. Frontier and pioneer life—Fiction.   2. Tennessee River—Fiction.
3. Adventure and adventurers—Fiction.]   I. Title.
PZ7.S8148Bu   2004
[Fic]—dc22   2004045353
ISBN 0-15-205214-3   ISBN 0-15-205215-1 (pb)

Printed in the United States of America

A C E G H F D B
A C E G H F D B (pb)

To my wife

Introduction

Anyone familiar with William O. Steele knows that in spite of all the close calls, his heroes come out all right in the end. Still, the suspense is so excruciating you can't help but wonder: How can he get out of *this* scrape? Will he make it? You never anticipate what is going to happen, but when it does happen, you not only believe, you worry. So it is when nine-year-old Andy Clark, his family, and the neighboring Brown family travel on a flatboat down one thousand miles of the Tennessee River to make a new home. They run into all the expected dangers from the river and a few unexpected as well: an attack by Indians, an encounter with a rattlesnake, and a near drowning.

Mr. Steele's books have another common characteristic. His hero may end up safe, but not without changing on the way. He is not the same boy at the close of the book as he was at the beginning. The adventures are not just meant to be overcome; they also leave a mark that makes a boy look at life somewhat differently. As this journey commences, Andy is rather hotheaded and careless, with a decided view of what makes a person acceptable. His own hero is his Uncle Az, a Long Hunter, a man of action, a lover of the outdoors, a teller of tall tales. At the other end of the scale is young Isaac Brown, who has just come back from a year in the city, working in his uncle's store. Isaac actually *prefers* city living to country living, and Andy has to be cooped up with him all the way down the Tennessee!

William Steele pilots a plot as deftly as he does a flatboat. And as swiftly. When you are through with these adventures, you will want to turn around and start over so you can take your time and enjoy the scenery.

Mr. Steele not only writes a good story, he writes good history that accurately reflects the feelings, the worries, the dangers of the times. And the language. When he refers to Native Americans as "redskins" or "savages," the reader understands that he finds these terms as objectionable as we do; he is simply recording what his characters would really have said. Only a skillful writer can tell a story that is true to *its* times and wind up with a truth that speaks to *all* times.

—Jean Fritz

The **Buffalo Knife**

1

"Andrew! Andrew Clark, where are you?"

"Yes'm, Ma, here I am," answered Andrew, coming out of the serviceberry bushes, followed by his old hound dog, Silas.

His mother smiled. "I declare, Andy, sometimes I think you and that dog are growed together. Can't one move without the other."

Andrew grinned and the dog pressed against his leg.

"Here," Mrs. Clark went on, handing him a wooden bucket. "Go down to the spring and fetch me this piggin full of water. And come right back. There's plenty you can do here."

Andy took the wooden piggin and started off to the spring. The little path was green with moss, and the bushes along it were covered with tiny new green leaves. Andrew and Silas sniffed at the pleasant, woodsy, springtime smell as they trotted down into the hollow.

At the bottom of the hollow a great oak tree spread over the little spring. The water bubbled up, clear and sparkling from between two rocks. Andrew and the hound lay down and drank together. The water was cold and sweet, not like some springs Andy had tasted with a bitter tang of iron or a sickening smell of sulphur.

He filled his piggin and set it down while he ran over to the little pool the spring made when it swirled around the oak tree. Across one side of the pool floated a thin jelly full of frog's eggs. Andrew counted the tadpoles. Twelve new ones since he had been here this noon!

He ran back to pick up his bucket, and as he stooped for it, he noticed Silas staring up the hill on the other side of the spring, his ears cocked and his tail still. Andy listened hard. Who was coming? Suppose it was—Indians!

Lots of times he'd heard of Indians hiding by a spring to catch boys who came down for water. For a minute he was so scared he couldn't move a muscle, he just stayed leaning over with his hand braced on the piggin handle. Then he straightened up. What a tom-fool he'd been. Silas would have barked if he'd smelled an Indian. It must be the dog had seen a squirrel or a rabbit.

No, someone was coming, but someone who was whistling softly and carrying a piggin like himself. It was Isaac Brown, coming for water.

"Hi," said Isaac.

"Hi," answered Andy. He was a little shy with Isaac. Although Isaac's father's land ran beside Andrew's father's fields, the two boys had never been friendly. During the two years the Browns had been neighbors of the Clarks, Isaac had been away in Salisbury for a good part of the time. When he was at home, he was too busy helping his pa to play much with other boys. Isaac was the oldest of the Brown children. Andy was thankful for his older brother and sister, who did most of the chores.

Isaac was ten, nearly a year older than Andrew. Last winter they had gone to the field schoolmaster's together to learn their letters. Isaac was quick at his books, Andrew remembered, but he was good at running and wrestling, too. Just as the two boys had begun to get acquainted, Isaac's uncle had come from Salisbury and taken his nephew to town with him again. Isaac had returned only two weeks ago.

Now things were different. From tomorrow on, Isaac and Andrew would have to be best friends. In fact they would be only friends for the next few months. Tomorrow Isaac's family and Andrew's family, with all their belongings including the dogs and pigs and chickens, would go aboard the big flatboat Mr. Clark and Mr. Brown had built, and sail down the Tennessee River.

Tomorrow they would begin the long and dangerous voyage to the French Salt Lick to make their homes one thousand miles away from the Holston River settlement. It gave Andy the shivers just thinking about it. His hands felt hot and cold with excitement. He didn't know how he'd ever *wait* till tomorrow morning.

"You folks all ready?" asked Andrew, feeling grown-up.

"We're all ready," said Isaac, and he stooped and filled his piggin.

Isaac set the water down and, reaching inside his shirt, drew out his knife. He opened it and going over to the big oak tree began to work on the place where he had carved his initials and the date on the trunk of the tree—*I. B. 1782*. He pushed the steel blade deep into the wood as though he wanted to make sure the marks stayed on that tree a long time.

Andrew watched enviously. More than anything in the world he wanted a knife of his own, a knife to whittle and carve and skin rabbits with, one he could heave at trees and Indians. He didn't want a pocketknife with a folding blade like Isaac's; he wanted a long shining hunting knife like the one his Uncle Aswell, who was a Long Hunter, carried.

To keep himself from thinking about the knife he began to talk about the trip. "Isaac, reckon we'll see many Chickamauga Indians when we get down to the Great Bend? Reckon there'll be any shooting?"

"I don't care," said Isaac gruffly.

"Don't care? What's the matter?" asked Andrew.

"I don't want to go," said Isaac, turning his head away.

"Don't want to go?" Andy was astonished. He simply could not believe it. "You mean you don't want to go down the Tennessee and see the Chickamaugas and Muscle Shoals and all the new country at French Salt Lick?"

"No," said Isaac shortly. "I want to go to Salisbury and live with my uncle. He wants me to come. He's got a store there, and he'd learn me to be a storekeeper if I'd come. I already know a heap about it."

Isaac turned, then, with sparkling eyes to Andrew and spoke with enthusiasm. "You ought to see what he's got in his store. Furs, and cloth dyed every color you can think of, and all the sugar you could eat, and guns and knives and hatchets. And things you ain't never seen—glass for windows, clocks to tell the time by, and dishes that ain't made out of wood or pewter. That's a fine sight, I can tell you."

"You mean you'd want to live in Salisbury? In a *town?*" asked Andrew.

"You ain't never been there," said Isaac. "You don't know what a fine thing it is to walk on a street, instead of slipping on a muddy old cowpath. And houses, setting as close to each other as I am to you, and a church and a schoolhouse, and . . . and . . . and a real jail!"

"I wouldn't like it," said Andrew firmly. "I like to be out in the woods, and I can't hardly wait till I'm big enough to go out and shoot me a deer or a bear."

"It's all right to live in the woods," answered Isaac, "but me, I want to get to town and get some real book-learning and *be* somebody."

"Well, why don't you go, then?" demanded Andy.

Isaac straightened his shoulders and looked serious and older. "Because my pa needs me. I'm the oldest at my house and my pa'll need help when he goes to a new place and starts clearing fields and building a cabin." He stooped for his piggin. "I got to go."

"Me, too," said Andrew, remembering his mother's warning to come right back. He scooted up his path without looking back at Isaac going up the other way.

There was a horse tied to the sycamore tree by the front door when Andy got back to the cabin. He almost spilled the water hurrying to get in. That was Sal, his Uncle Aswell's mare.

Andrew reckoned nobody ever had an uncle like his Uncle Aswell. Maybe if Isaac's uncle had been like Uncle Aswell, Isaac would have known how much better it was to live in the woods than in the town—how much freer and cleaner and more exciting and, well, better. When Uncle Aswell talked about the Long Hunts he made, about Indians and about the forests and rivers, it was almost more than Andrew could do to stay home and sleep in his bed.

He wanted to be off down the trails, into the woods. He wanted to go where white men had never gone before, and come home to tell the others of sights he had seen, great rivers and mountains, plains where buffalo and deer grazed in herds of thousands. Oh, the tales Uncle Az could tell of game he had seen and shot and trapped!

Andy's mother met him at the door and took the piggin. "Mercy on us, Andrew. You were gone such a time I made sure a catamount had you. Come in and speak to your Uncle Aswell."

Andy did not need to be told. "Uncle Az, Uncle Az!" he yelled, flinging himself on the tall young man with the brown beard who sat by the table.

Uncle Aswell laughed and grabbed Andy's hair with one big hard hand and pulled it gently.

"How many bears you shot since I seen you last?" he asked teasingly.

"About a thousand, I reckon," said Andrew. "I killed three or four down at the spring just now, just little bitty ones. That's how come I took so long," and he grinned at his mother.

"You ready to go down the river?" Uncle Aswell asked. Mrs. Clark set a plate full of food in front of him and he began to eat.

"I sure am," exclaimed Andy. "Why don't you come with us?"

"Why don't you come on the trail with me? We'd get there first."

"Now, Aswell," said Mrs. Clark. "Don't go putting notions in Andy's head. He's hard enough to hold down as it is."

"Your mammy thinks you're too young to go on the trail, lad," said Uncle Aswell sadly, shaking his head. "But anyway I got something for you, to help you fight the Indians."

He put down his knife and reached inside his hunting shirt. The shirt was so big that when it was belted around the middle, it bloused over the belt and made a fine place for carrying things. Uncle Aswell's shirt was always bumpy with his possessions. Now he pulled out his hands, doubled up so Andy couldn't see what was in them, and stuck them behind him.

"Which hand do you take?"

"That one," said Andrew, his eyes shining with excitement. Whatever Az had for him it would be good. He watched the big fist as it slowly unclenched, and there in the palm lay a brown twist of tobacco.

Andrew looked up in silent disappointment, and Aswell chuckled.

"You want me to chew it?" asked Andy, and his mother said quickly, "Aswell, don't you go letting him chew tobacco. Give him what you've got in your other hand."

"Why, sure now, Andy, here's the other."

He brought out his other hand with a hunting knife, stuck in a scabbard, in the open palm.

"Oh!" was all Andrew could say, but he grabbed the knife quickly.

"Now, young 'un, it's sharp so be careful as a killdee. I take it you know how to use a knife." Uncle Aswell watched him, and Andrew nodded.

"Mind your manners, son," said Mrs. Clark, and Andrew mumbled, "Thank you, Uncle Aswell. It's a fine knife."

"It's a pretty good one. The handle's made out of buffalo bones, shin bones."

"Did you kill the buffalo, Uncle Az?" asked Andy, hoping for a story.

"Of course I killed it. Spit 'bacco juice right in his eye. Why, I reckon I'm about the only man ever killed a buffalo," Uncle Aswell teased. "Looky yonder, there's your pappy coming with Ralph. Run meet 'em while I finish my dinner."

Andrew ran out, shouting and waving his new knife.

"Looky, Ralph, looky here!" he yelled.

"Looky what Uncle Az brought me. Ain't it fine? The handle's made out of buffalo bones."

His father laughed and caught Andy's arm as he stumbled up to him, so eager to show his new knife that he wouldn't watch where he was going.

"What in the nation is it? I reckon if you'd hold it still, a body might be able to tell what it was."

"A knife, a hunting knife!" Andy pulled the

knife from its leather sheath and held it out. "Ain't it a beauty?"

Ralph and Mr. Clark examined the knife carefully.

"It's a good knife, Andrew," said Mr. Clark. "You take care of it and it'll last you a lifetime."

"It's a lot better than mine," said Ralph, showing his. "Mine's just got a wood handle, and it ain't so keen."

Andy looked at the two knives. Of course, he knew his was the best, but he knew too that Ralph was trying to make him feel good. Ralph was going to the Lick by the dangerous overland trail with Uncle Aswell. With some other men they were going to drive the livestock through Kentucky and down to the Lick. The flatboat was too small to carry cows and enough feed for them. Ralph was fourteen, and Andy knew nine was too young to go on the trail. But still he couldn't help feeling he'd be just as handy as Ralph, and Ralph knew how keenly disappointed Andy was that he had to go by river.

So Ralph was specially nice to Andrew these days, letting Andy hold his rifle, and be the winner when they raced to the cowshed in the mornings, praising him for the way he quieted the horses, or handled the ax when they chopped wood.

"Where's Kate?"

"She stopped back a ways to pick some violets. Yonder she comes now," said Mr. Clark.

"Girls!" said Ralph and Andrew together in disgust, and they all laughed.

Kate admired the knife, too, when she came up. Andy had to admit she was a good sister. She could run mighty near as fast as Ralph, when nobody was looking, and she was strong.

In the house Uncle Aswell was playing with Peggy, who was five years old, the baby of the family. As they came in he looked up and said, "You are just in time to tell this young 'un I'm telling her the truth."

"Don't believe a word he says." Ralph laughed.

"Depends on what you've told," said Mr. Clark.

"Peggy here wants to know why I got this beard. I keep telling her I got my pet screech owl in there, and she won't believe me."

Uncle Aswell poked Peggy in the ribs and made her giggle.

Andy slipped up behind his uncle and grabbed his arms. "Pull his beard, Peggy, and let's see if it's real."

Uncle Aswell struggled and pretended he could not get loose from Andy. As Peggy climbed into his lap, he jerked his head every which way and begged and moaned.

"Don't, Peggy. Oh-h-h."

But Peggy reached quickly up and grabbed a fistful of Aswell's beard and yanked with all her might.

"Ouch and thunderation!" cried Az painfully. Ralph and Mr. Clark laughed aloud, and Peggy said soberly to Andy, "I can't tell is it real, Andy. It won't come off."

2

"A good Long Hunter's got to take care with his feet," said Aswell as he sewed up a split in his moccasin. "Don't forget that, Andy. Take care of your feet and they'll take care of you."

Andy squatted beside his uncle, watching his big brown hands move so skillfully. He sighed. He'd never be able to do things the way Aswell did. There wasn't anything Aswell couldn't fix or anything he couldn't make. He was a real woodsman, able to care for himself for months at a time out in the forest with only his rifle and his knife. Sometimes Aswell was gone for a year or more on a Long Hunt, and when he came home, he never stayed but a few days. He didn't like cabins and lots of people fussing around. But all the time he was home, Andy never left him if he could help it. Now he brought out the buffalo bone knife and balanced it in his hand.

"Uncle Az, did you ever kill a Cherokee with a knife?"

"Not a Cherokee," he answered firmly. "A Chickamauga, maybe, but the Cherokees are my friends. I don't fight 'em."

Andy was surprised. "Ralph said Chickamaugas and Cherokee Indians were the same thing."

"No, they ain't," Aswell told him. "The Cherokee Indians are friendly to the white men. They live up on the Little Tennessee and don't hardly ever give any trouble. All the Indians that didn't want to be friends with the white men left the Cherokee Nation, and they're the ones we call the Chickamaugas—along with some no-good Indians from other tribes, runaway slaves, and even some white men that are just plain mean and shiftless."

Az looked into Andy's eyes and said, "They all live down there by the Chickamauga Creek near the Suck like a bunch of rattlesnakes and you can kill any one you see." He returned to his work.

"Well, *did* you ever kill a Chickamauga?"

"Not with a knife as I recollect," Aswell answered. "Once I was near enough to Dragging Canoe, the Chief of the Chickamaugas, to kill him. But I didn't figure it was a healthy thing to do. I was a-visiting in a Cherokee town and Dragging Canoe came there to talk with his brother. He's a great tall Indian, with scars on his face."

"Do you reckon the British are still supplying the Chickamaugas with guns and powder?" inquired Mr. Clark.

"I reckon they are," Aswell answered. "They're keeping the redskins stirred up like a bunch of hornets—not that the Chickamaugas need much stirring up. They hate the white men and they always will. They don't want to see him settle in this valley, and I don't know as I blame 'em. I'd hate mighty bad to see roads and cabins all through there myself."

Aswell grinned and Andy grinned back. That was a funny notion, cabins and houses in those thick dark forests! Why, it would be a thousand years, he reckoned, before folks settled all the way down the Tennessee Valley. Some day Americans would live there though. They had already run the British out of this country, just about, and some day the Indians would leave, too. Then men like his Uncle Az, the brave and reckless Long Hunters, would range all through that land and find the best places for people to settle and start new towns, just as Andy and his family were going now to the new settlement at the French Salt Lick.

"Do you think we'll have trouble with them,

then?" Mrs. Clark broke into Andy's thoughts.

"No," Aswell answered. "You shouldn't have trouble with the Indians or the rocks either in this high water." He looked around at all of them. "I don't mean it'll be an easy lay-a-bed journey. There'll be danger and work a plenty."

Mrs. Clark sighed. "I know, and I dread to go."

Andy looked at his mother in surprise. Her voice was so grave and troubled. He had not stopped to think whether his mother really wanted to make this river journey or not. He was so eager to go himself, he had simply assumed that the whole family was as anxious to start as he was.

"Oh, I reckon you'll get through in fine shape," Aswell spoke cheerfully. "The spring rain'll make the current so high and fast that you'll be there 'fore you know it. And, Andy, that's real country over there. Flat rich land, so a body could raise a crop without hardly trying. And game! Great thunderation! Buffalo so thick you can walk for miles on their backs without touching the ground."

"Now, Uncle Az," chided Kate, while Andy leaned on his uncle's knee, dreaming of the great woolly beasts grazing over the savannahs.

"It's a fact," Aswell answered. "Just walk along on their backs and count out which one you want to kill.

> '*Una, doona, tree,*
> *Let this one be.*
> *Lead, lime, muzzlelock,*
> *Kill the next one in the flock.*'

And knock that one in the head."

"Uncle Az," said Andy, breathless. "Do you reckon I could kill a buffalo with my new knife?"

"Well, I don't know now. You might kill a snapping turtle. There's a lot of folks say snapping turtles are the most dangerous varmints on earth."

He looked solemnly at his nephew. "You keep a sharp eye out for turtles on the way down the Tennessee. Don't you go fooling around 'em. Why, in the spring of '78 one of the fool things grabbed a-holt of my toe, and it was dang near the end of me."

Andy listened seriously.

"Now you know a snapping turtle won't let loose till it thunders. He bit me in June and the two of us sat around all summer waiting for some thunder. I never knew thunder to be so scarce. Long 'bout one day in September that turtle must of been getting wore out, 'cause he opened his jaws and asked me wasn't that thunder he heard, and I just naturally didn't wait to answer him."

"Aw," said Andy and they all laughed, but Aswell shook his head solemnly. "Why, them things are more dangerous than all the rocks and shoals in the river. I've known four of 'em to lie in wait for a flatboat and grab it by the four corners and pull it down under the water just by sheer orneriness."

"I don't want to go where those mean old turtles are," Peggy said tearfully.

Uncle Az picked her up. "Honey, I was just a-fooling. And there ain't a turtle in the whole river would hurt a sweet thing like you, don't you know it?"

Ralph went outside, and Kate said, "Ma, look at Andy. Be you going to let him sit there on the floor and not raise his hand? He'll let Ralph do everything."

Andy scrambled to his feet and ran from the room to help Ralph coop up the chickens. He wasn't going to stay in there and listen to Kate nag. Out in the warm spring sun, it felt good to run with Ralph and chase the chickens in and out of the huckleberry bushes.

He pretended he was chasing deer and buffalo, and maybe even Chickamaugas. He could feel his beautiful new knife against his side, and he wondered how it would feel to thrust that sharp blade between a buffalo's great ribs. He wondered if he'd get a chance to use his knife on the voyage down the river.

He stopped under a sycamore tree, thinking about

the voyage, the Indians, the dangers, the excitements, and the new land of hope and plenty, where they were going. He was glad his father had decided to go. This was good country, but it was hilly and heavily wooded. Land was hard to clear, harder to plow. At the French Salt Lick, they claimed a man could buy, for very little money, land that would make him rich. A man could raise a crop or pasture a cow without cutting down all the trees in creation. No steep hillsides there, only rolling meadows. His thoughts were interrupted when Ralph came up with the old rooster under his arm.

"Ralph," said Andy, "would you tell me something? Don't tell Az I don't know. But what is the Suck?"

Ralph grinned. "It's a place where you have to get out and tote the flatboats on your back, else you get sucked down to the bottom of the river."

"Aw, Ralph, what is it sure enough?"

"It's just a bad stretch in the river, where it has to go between a heap of mountains and it gets narrow and fast, and the way's full of shoals and rocks. Uncle Az says it's not bad in high water. Anyway, that's where the Chickamaugas have their towns and the fast current is a help to get by them." Ralph added loftily, "It ain't really dangerous like it is going by land through Kentuck."

"I reckon not," said Andy, downcast. He helped Ralph stuff the rooster and the four hens in the coop, and then he went on into the house. He looked around at the little cabin. In another few hours they would be gone from here forever. He felt tired and sort of lonesome, and he wished he could get a chance to talk to Aswell again, but his mother and Kate put him to work.

He ran his legs off, carrying the last deer hide full of jerked meat for Ralph to tie up, the last bundles of quilts and cooking skillets and clothes. Somehow the coop got turned over and two of the hens got out and he had to chase them. Supper was just cold ash cake and milk, and Andy was so tired he could hardly eat his. He sat on the pile of bundles that Ralph and Uncle Aswell would take with them in the morning, holding his ash cake in his hand and listening to the talk.

His ma was telling Ralph to take his hunting shirt off if it got wet and not let it dry on him, Aswell was telling his pa about the land at the French Salt Lick, how flat and rich and green it was, and Pa was marveling at it, saying over and over again that it was just what he wanted, he could hardly wait to start clearing his fields.

Andrew didn't know he was asleep till his mother shook him and said, "Get up, Andy; we're leaving."

He was in his own bed. It was still pitch-dark, and he was still half asleep. He hardly knew how he got out of bed and stumbled by candlelight across the floor and helped gather up the last of the baggage and put it in the wagon. He went to sleep again in the wagon with Silas beside him, but he woke up properly when they went on board the flatboat.

The sky was beginning to lighten now, and Andrew could hear the river rushing down over the rocks and feel it tug at the great boat. By the time they were all aboard and their belongings put away, he was wide awake. And by the time Mr. Brown untied the boat and climbed on board, and Mr. Clark began to shove with the pole to get the boat out in the current, he remembered his knife.

"Looky here, Isaac," he said. "Uncle Az brought me a hunting knife."

He began to feel in his shirt, remembering that he had slipped it in there last night. He reached and felt all around. But the knife was gone!

Andrew felt inside his shirt again. He knew he had put the knife in there last night. Or maybe he had left it lying by that stump when he cut Peggy a little wooden spoon for her dolly last night. But surely he remembered picking up the knife. He'd been so tired and sleepy by the time supper was ready, he didn't rightly know what he'd done. Could he have lost his precious hunting knife?

"Wait a peg, Isaac, I'll find it," he muttered.

He could hear his father and Isaac's talking as they moved the boat with poles away from the shore and into the river current. Andy staggered a little when the flatboat swung out into the stream, and he looked toward shore. In the half-light he could see Ralph and Aswell waving from the bank, and he waved back. He wanted to holler for them to run back and look for his knife, but he hated for Aswell to know he'd been careless and lost his buffalo-bone knife.

The current was strong and swift for the spring rains and melting snows had flooded into the river, and almost before Andrew knew it, Uncle Az and Ralph were out of sight. He felt lonely and sad, instead of excited and happy the way he'd expected to feel. He was going down the Tennessee River to a strange place, through many dangers, leaving behind the cabin that had been his home as far back as he could remember, the places and people he had known so long. And worst of all, he had lost his hunting knife.

Halfheartedly he searched inside his shirt again. Isaac watched mockingly.

"Let's see the knife," said Isaac. "I reckon you swallowed it."

"I got it someplace," answered Andy, trying desperately to think what he could have done with it. But he *knew* he'd put it in his shirt. The last thing he remembered doing last night was to feel for his knife.

"I reckon I lost it," he confessed miserably at last. "It was a hunting knife, a real one with a deer-hide sheath, and the handle was made out of buffalo bones. My Uncle Aswell gave it to me." He thought a minute. "Maybe I dropped it in the wagon on the way to the boat."

"Maybe you dropped it in the river when you come on board," said Isaac cruelly. "Maybe some old crawdad has run off with it."

"Maybe Ma has it for me," remarked Andy, looking brighter. "I bet she fetched it along for me."

"Maybe your Uncle Az stole it from you," jeered Isaac. "I reckon he's an Injun giver. Maybe you just made all that up. I reckon you just never had you a knife at all." And he brushed sullenly by Andrew and went and sat near where his father was working the long paddle-sweep with which the boat was steered.

Andrew stared after him in amazement. Now what was making Isaac so feisty?

He, Andrew, was the one who had lost a good knife, the knife he had wanted so long and hadn't hoped to have till he was as old as Ralph. And now most likely they wouldn't let him have another till he was a man grown, eighteen years old and old enough to have a rifle and go out in the woods on his own. He sighed and climbed down onto the deck of the flatboat.

The boat was really a huge raft made of split logs. Its front was sloping, slanted from the top to the waterline. A flat-roofed cabin took up the rear half of the raft, and from the top of this cabin the men did all the steering and poling. The deck in front of the cabin was enclosed with a wooden wall higher than Andy's head, so if he wanted to see anything, he had to go up on the cabin roof. On this lower enclosed deck were the crude pens for the dogs and pigs and chickens. Andrew went up to the pen where Silas lay with his nose on his paws looking mournfully about.

"Maybe we'll just get off this old boat tonight, Silas, and strike out through the woods, you and me," Andy whispered through the pen slats.

"That'd be fine, wouldn't it? We could catch up with Ralph and Uncle Az and go with them."

He thought about it a little, because it was fun to think about, but he knew he'd never be able to do it. Specially now that he had no knife to defend himself against bears and Indians. He sighed again and stood up. He hated to go tell his ma he'd lost the knife, but he had to know whether she had it. Likely not. If she'd found it, she'd sure have given it to him. She had enough to do without carrying his truck around.

"I'll ask Pa can I let you out in a little while, Silas," he whispered to the dog and Silas thumped his tail in answer.

He went into the cabin. It was dark inside, for there were no windows. There was a big stone fireplace at one end, and his mother knelt beside it, cleaning off the ash board and placing the cornmeal cake on it to bake.

Andrew watched her and smelled the good smell that came from the pot hanging over the fire. All of a sudden he was so hungry he could hardly stand it. But he had to know about the knife. He looked over to where his sister Kate was spreading quilts out on the bunks that ran along the walls. He didn't want Kate to know he'd lost his knife. His ma wouldn't fuss at him, but Kate would.

"Ma," he said softly. "You ain't seen my new knife, the one Uncle Az gave me?"

"No, I ain't," she answered, looking up. "Andrew, did you lose that good knife?"

"I . . . I just can't remember where I put it, Ma," Andy stammered.

"Well, what's gone is gone. But it'll be a long, long time before you get another. I'd a-thought a boy nine years old could take better care of things than that."

She stirred the stew and then she turned to him and smiled. "Go tell the menfolks to come eat. And don't fret over the knife; worrying won't help none.

Just remember next time to put things in their proper places."

He stood on the deck, cupped his hands and shouted, "Pa, Ma says come eat!" He was feeling so bad, he doubted if he could have eaten anything, except he was so hungry. He managed to eat two helpings of stew and ash cake, and then he felt better.

He looked over at Isaac, and Isaac had taken out his jackknife and was showing Peggy and David, Isaac's little brother, how to play mumblety-peg. The knife blade quivered in the puncheon floor. Kate was feeding Sophronia, Isaac's baby sister. Mrs. Brown and Mrs. Clark were still eating, and Mr. Brown was just finishing.

Andy's father had stayed on the cabin roof to steer, and now Mr. Brown was going up to do the steering while Mr. Clark ate. He set his bowl down, and looked up suddenly.

"Listen," he said. "That must be Reedy Shoals."

The others all stopped and listened, too. Above the popping of the wood fire, they heard a steady roaring noise that grew gradually louder. The Shoals! Where the swift water churned over rocks that often lay only inches beneath the surface, treacherous and ugly.

Mr. Brown ran for the cabin door with Isaac and

Andy on his heels. Just as Andy stepped out of the door, there was a sudden crashing jolt and the boat ground against something. Andy reeled across the deck and fell against the chicken pen and all the hens began to cackle and holler, the pigs began to squeal, and the dogs to bark. The womenfolks all screamed, and Phronie, the baby, began to cry.

You could hardly hear the roar of the shallow water rushing over the rocks for all the noise on the boat. Andy thought his head was going to split open. He scrambled up and followed Isaac and Mr. Brown onto the roof. Mr. Brown was talking to Andy's father when Andy finally got up on top, and Isaac ran back and hollered down to his mother, "The flatboat's on a rock, Ma, but Mr. Clark don't think we're stuck. We'll soon have her off."

Now don't he think he's big? Andy asked himself. *Telling everybody what's what.*

He stayed near the roof edge, waiting, not wanting to go over where Isaac stood by the two men. On the deck, Mrs. Brown calmed the baby. Kate commanded the dogs to be quiet, and the chickens subsided into indignant clucks. Now the sound of the shoals was loud and steady and fierce, so that Andy could hardly hear his father's shout.

"Get a pole, son. You'll have to help push us off."

Andy jumped down and handed up the poles which were laid ready for just such an emergency as this. He clambered back on the roof and ran over to the place at one side where his father pointed.

He moved his pole along the river bottom till he could feel it wedge tight against something. They would all push together on the side where the boat had run up on the rock. At a signal from his father, Andy leaned on his pole and pushed with all his might. The muscles in his arms ached and his eyes felt ready to pop out with the strain. But still the boat stuck fast.

"A little less grunt and more git there, boy," smiled Mr. Clark, and they pushed once more.

"Hold on," said Mr. Brown. "Let's tote the boxes and stuff over to the other side. That'll lighten this side and maybe she'll float free."

They laid down the poles and set to work. Even Kate helped carry the baggage across to the other side of the deck. The smaller children watched wide-eyed and Andy was glad his father thought he was old enough and strong enough to help.

They picked up the poles and shoved again. Andy was discouraged, and he suddenly felt they might just as well give up and stay right here and not try to go to the French Salt Lick. But he gave one more heave, along with the others, and the boat floated free, grating off the rock, then scraping and rocking down the shoals.

The back end suddenly swung around, so that the boat began to go sidewise down the river. Mr. Brown ran for the steering paddle. He leaned against it trying to get the front part of the boat pointed downstream. Mr. Clark came up to help him, and Isaac and Andy stood side by side holding their poles and looking helplessly down into the foamy swirling river.

Ahead rocks showed dangerously through the white churning water. Isaac pointed to the rapids, and he looked white and scared. "Looky yonder, Andy. You reckon a flatboat can turn over?"

Andy grinned to himself. Isaac was scared. "Naw. This ain't nothing. Wait till we get to Muscle Shoals. Then you'll really see some rocks. And how about the place they call the Suck, downriver?" He looked at Isaac out of the corner of his eye. "Can't you swim, Isaac?"

"Not very good," answered Isaac. And then he turned and faced Andy. "But I ain't scared. Maybe I just got a little old *pocket*knife instead of a hunting knife, but I ain't scared a mite."

Mr. Clark and Mr. Brown were still trying to turn the boat in water so shallow that the rocks continually scraped the logs of the flatboat. But the current was so swift that they shot through the rapids and shoals almost before they knew it. Then they were drifting in a pool of quiet water. Mr. Clark turned the boat till the front end was downstream.

The two men sat down on the rooftop and wiped their faces. After a while Mr. Clark called Andy over and said, "Here, son, you and Isaac steer awhile. The river's pretty straight now. I got to help Mr. Brown move the things back where they belong. Then I'm going to eat. I'm hungry enough to eat a settlement of bears."

Andy grabbed the steering paddle, a long pole with a broad blade on one end and the other end resting in the crotch of the forked branch fastened to the cabin roof.

"Now don't let go the pole and let it slide in the water," cautioned Mr. Brown. "Pull it up on the roof if you want to quit steering."

Isaac watched awhile as Andy moved the paddle in the water. Andy squinted his eyes at the river ahead and made a great show of avoiding rocks.

"I heard tell about a flatboat run on a rock near Chickamauga territory, and every lasting soul aboard got scalped, except those that got knocked off the boat and drowned," Andy told Isaac.

He had the older boy at a disadvantage now and he was going to get even for Isaac's meanness earlier in the day. He would tell all the scary things he knew about river journeys and let Isaac worry a little.

Isaac had decided not to scare easy, however. "I reckon if you'd been there, you'd have rode ashore on that knife you say you got, and cut your way through the whole tarnal Indian nation."

Andy was cheerful. "Might have now. I reckon I'd of killed a heap of them Chickamaugas when I got ashore. You can do lots with a hunting knife. Now a town man, all he needs is a pocketknife. But a Long Hunter needs a real knife that's some use."

He added politely, "I'd let you steer awhile, Isaac, but you might get scared if you saw a rock coming at us. Town boys don't know about woods and rivers."

"I ain't scared!" Isaac shouted. "You give me that paddle, I'll show you."

He grabbed at the paddle, shoving at Andy with his elbow. The younger boy clutched at the pole, missed it, stumbled, and threw up his arms. He had a glimpse of Isaac's startled face and then he hurtled backward, too surprised even to yell when the icy roaring river closed over him.

4

For a moment Andy saw the edge of the flatboat against the cloudy sky. And then the freezing water closed over him, pushing its way into his ears and nose and eyes. He gasped and swallowed a muddy mouthful. He struck out with his arms, but still he went down, down, down forever.

Finally, the bottom came up under his feet and he thrashed about with his legs and arms and began to rise. His ears rang and his nose ached with the cold water, his lungs began to burn for air. He was going to drown. He knew it as sure as shooting. In his mind's eye, he saw his own limp body dragged down by the current and forever hid from sight.

He gave a despairing kick with his legs and burst out into the air. He drew a great sobbing breath, and then fought to keep his head out of the water. The current pulled at his legs and the ripples rushed by his ears with a dizzying roaring noise. He couldn't seem to get enough air into his lungs, and he couldn't see the boat.

He moved his arms weakly trying to swim, and then he heard his father shout, "Andy, grab the paddle."

Andrew saw the long blade reaching toward him. The current seemed to be getting swifter, and his clothes hung on him like dead weights. He grabbed at the steering paddle, but he couldn't seem to get his hands out of the water. The river bore him swiftly along, he didn't have to bother to try to swim now, but he knew they were coming to another rapids. He *had* to grab the paddle before the rushing water carried him in among the rocks and beat him to pieces.

Voices called frantically, "Grab the paddle, Andy. Grab the paddle," and he lunged again for the flat wooden blade.

He had the slippery thing in his hands, but it was sliding from his grasp. He clutched desperately and then the flatboat shot away from him, rocking down the rapids. Andy could see the rocks coming toward him and the swirling white foam. He headed straight for a big black rock and then suddenly he was tossed another way and went rolling underwater, bumping another rock as he went.

For a few minutes, he rolled and slithered and

bumped with terrifying speed, gasping and choking, sometimes out of the shallow water and sometimes sliding on the rock bottom. He was too sick and dizzy to care what happened to him. He swallowed more water than he had thought the whole river held. And then suddenly he fell out into the quiet place below the rapids and strong arms reached for him and somebody gave him something to drink that burned all through him. His head ached terribly and he was so tired and sleepy he could have gone to sleep that minute, but somebody grabbed him up and the next thing he knew he was in bed with a million quilts, it felt like, on top of him. Then almost at once he was asleep.

He woke a while later and his father was bending over him. "Ain't no bones broken," Mr. Clark said, running his hands over Andy's legs. "Andy, how in the nation did you come to fall off the roof?"

He didn't wait for an answer but turned away, saying, "You always was lucky though. I mind that time you fell out of the hickory tree. I made sure you was dead, and all you got was some scratches."

Mrs. Clark smiled at Andy and held out a bowl to him. He drank the good warm broth, and then sank back beneath the quilts, already half asleep. But as he drifted off, he wondered what Isaac would say when they asked *him* how Andy came to fall off the roof.

When Andy woke again he knew it was morning. Even in the cabin it had the chill feel of early morning. He lay back in bed feeling rested and fine and sorry he'd missed most of the first day on the river. He looked around and saw that the cabin was empty except for Mrs. Brown fussing over Sophronia across the room, and his own mother sitting near him in a chair doing some mending.

"Ma," he said, "can I get up?"

"I reckon so, son," she answered. "That is, if you think you can stay on the boat."

She reached over and laid her hand on his cheek. "You ain't got a fever. I'll rub you with grease tonight, and I reckon you'll make it all right."

Andy threw back the quilts and sat up, but he stopped instantly. He was so sore and stiff he could hardly move. He could see a great blue bruise all down his left arm and the skin on his legs from knee to ankle was scraped almost off. It wouldn't do to let his mother see how bad off he was, so he waited till she turned back to her sewing and then he eased himself out of bed, moving cautiously and slowly.

His mother said without looking up, "Get some of that bear grease out of the gourd by the hearth there, Andy, and rub it on your legs. It'll help a heap."

Andy glanced at her. She saw everything. A boy had to be a mile away in the middle of a willow grove before he got where she couldn't see him.

While he was rubbing the grease on his legs, Mrs. Clark brought him a plate of food. Mrs. Brown came over and rubbed his head and told him to watch his step today.

Peggy leaned against him and asked, "Did you see a fish, Andy?"

Andy laughed. "If there was any fishes around there, I didn't have time to see 'em. I reckon I did some fast traveling."

He stood up and handed his empty trencher to his mother. "Where's Isaac?"

"Out with the menfolks."

Mrs. Clark said, "Now you watch yourself today, Andrew. Don't go falling off again. Next time you may not be so lucky."

Andy frowned going out the cabin door. Did they really think he'd just fallen off the roof? A woodsman like Andrew Clark had to be surer-footed than that. Had Isaac told them what had really happened or had he told them Andy just fell off?

Outside, his sister Kate was feeding the chickens and pigs. Silas followed at her heels, but when he saw Andy he bounded over to the boy and jumped around him, whining joyfully.

"Reckon you're glad to get out, boy," said Andrew, rubbing the dog's ears, and remembering how he'd promised yesterday to let him out.

Kate said, "Well, Andy, are you aiming to go swimming this morning?"

Andrew didn't answer, and Kate reached in her pocket and took something out. She put it in his hand and then gave his arm a squeeze and told him, "I'm glad you didn't drown."

Andy grinned at her and began to eat the handful of hickory nut meats she had given him. Kate was all right. She was just bossy sometimes. He climbed up on the cabin roof, though he was so stiff and sore he could hardly make it, and walked over to where his father and Mr. Brown and Isaac stood by the steering paddle.

Mr. Brown said, "Well, Andy, you going to stick to the boat, or you think you can get there faster swimming?"

"How do you feel, son?" asked Mr. Clark.

"Fine," said Andy and he gave Isaac a long look. What had the other boy told?

As if in answer to his question, Mr. Clark said, "Just what did happen? We got so excited yesterday, we plumb forgot to ask."

Andy opened his mouth and then shut it. So Isaac hadn't said anything. Of course Andy wasn't going to tattle and say Isaac pushed him. Besides he would have to confess he had been teasing Isaac and keeping the steering paddle from him.

Finally he said slowly, "I don't rightly know. I was just getting ready to give the steering paddle to Isaac, and we got sort of tangled up and I fell off."

He looked up at his father. It was just about the truth, but he hated to have his father think he'd been clumsy and careless.

Mr. Brown spoke up. "You have to watch the paddle. In these rough places it can strike a rock, or a current can hit it and jerk it right smart. I reckon that's what happened, Andy, and it throwed you off. It's our fault for leaving you young 'uns up here alone. From now on, one of us'll stay by while you two steer. That way you can get the hang of it without any more trouble."

He winked at Andy, and Andy nodded. It was all right. He hadn't gotten Isaac in trouble, and the men didn't think he'd been woodenheaded. He sat down on the flat roof. The spring sun felt good on his back, and his muscles were beginning to loosen up some now.

Presently Isaac came and sat by him. When the

two men were busy, Isaac said in a low tone, "I'm sorry, Andy. I never went to make you fall."

"I know it," said Andy. "No harm's done."

Isaac was silent a minute, and then suddenly he held out his hand with his knife lying in it. "Here, you can keep it for today."

Andrew stared down at the knife in Isaac's hand. He longed to pick it up and unfold the blade, to keep it and use it and play as if it was his own. But he did not touch it. Isaac needn't think he could make up that way. That was a town boy's trick, Andy thought scornfully. He didn't need pay just because he hadn't told on Isaac.

"I don't want it," he muttered. "I got no use for it. A pocketknife's no good out in the woods."

Isaac drew back his hand with the knife. He hesitated a moment as though he was about to speak and then he got up suddenly and went off. Andy stayed where he was. In his heart he knew Isaac had offered the knife to show that he was willing to be friends, to forget all the past and start over. It was the sight of the knife and reminder of the loss of his own that had made Andy ugly. He sighed, wondering where he'd lost it. His beautiful knife.

Of course, Isaac couldn't understand how bad losing his knife made him feel, any more than Andy could understand how Isaac would prefer going to Salisbury instead of to the French Salt Lick. He pondered a minute. He reckoned now he knew why Isaac had been so mean yesterday when they were leaving, just like he'd been so mean a minute ago because he hated losing his knife.

But why in the nation would any boy want to live in the town? It must be that Isaac was *afraid* to live in the woods with bears and Indians all about. He shook his head. He couldn't ever be real friends with a boy like that. He was glad he hadn't taken the pocketknife.

5

Andy sat beside the fireplace, listening to the rain beating on the roof and the wind blowing against the cabin door. Near about a million gallons of water had fallen on that cabin roof in the past three days, he reckoned. He was so weary of the noise, he was 'most ready to give up and swim back up the river to his old home.

He rolled over away from the fire to watch the younger children. Sophronia was beating on the floor with a wooden spoon. She seemed happy. Dan and Peggy were playing in a corner. Peggy was crawling around on her hands and knees, going in a circle around Dan who stood stiffly with his hands at his sides.

Andy went a little nearer to see what they were doing, but Peggy stopped crawling and looked at him, big-eyed.

"What in the nation are you doin'?" asked Andrew.

The two little ones looked at him, and finally Dan said, "Peggy here's a calf and she's done been tethered to a post, and I be the post."

"Oh, be you?" cried Andy. "Well, I be a big old fly and I'm going to sting that calf!" And he swooped down on Peggy with his fingers making pinching motions.

Peggy screamed and ran to her mother.

"Andrew!" said Mrs. Clark. "Be ashamed to tease the little ones, a big growed boy like you."

"You ain't got enough to do, that's how come you're so full of meanness," said Kate. "Here, take this piggin and help me feed the critters."

Andrew, grumbling, took the bucket and went out on the deck. The wind blew the water in gray sheets across the boat and the cold spring rain was sharp and chilling. By the time they had finished feeding the chickens and dogs and pigs, they were wet to the skin.

When Andy came in, his ma made him change clothes. She built up the fire to warm them and they all gathered close to the hearth, feeling the chill that came in with Kate and Andy.

Andy sat hugging his knees, enjoying the warmth,

watching the steam rise from his wet shirt where it hung by the fire. It was friendly and cozy. At home, he thought, they'd have nuts to crack or corn to pop, a wet evening like this. For a moment he was almost homesick.

Suddenly his ma got up and fetched a bag back to the hearth. "I knew I brought these scaly-barks along for some reason," she said, and smiled at Andy.

Soon they were cracking the nuts and digging out the sweet meats.

Kate sat by the fire combing her long hair to dry it, with Ma's cedar comb Pa had whittled for her. She combed it and combed it, till finally Andy said, "Kate's fixing to marry up with a fish. She's getting all prettied up to meet her feller, and she ain't likely to meet up with anybody much else than a fish out here in the river."

Kate pushed him with her foot. Mrs. Brown said, "Kate, I'll tell you how you can find out who you're going to marry."

"Well," said Andy, "you better tell her. A girl as ugly as Kate is sure going to have a hard time finding somebody to marry her." He moved away as he spoke so his sister couldn't reach him.

"On the first day of May you go to the spring

and fetch something shiny with you, like a pewter plate," said Mrs. Brown. "When the sun first comes up, let it hit that shiny thing so it throws a shadow in the spring. And there your true love's picture will be a-floating on the spring water."

Kate smiled at her mother. "Did you do that afore you got married up, Ma?"

Mr. Clark spoke up quickly, "She did. And she seen a wrinkled old possum looking up at her. That's me."

They all laughed, but Mr. Brown held up a hand and said soberly, "You may well laugh, but I 'member a girl lived near me once. She tried that trick in the spring and you know what she saw?"

"What?" asked Andy.

"A piece of wood that looked just like a bury-box. She laughed like you all did, and not a week later she was dead."

"Aw, Pa, you just made that up," said Isaac.

"Nosirree."

"Quit scaring the young 'uns," said Mrs. Brown. "Seems like you could find more to do than give them bad dreams."

"Oh, I know a story that'll make your hair stand on end," said Mr. Brown. "Once there was a stingy old man. And he heard tell if'n you'd set a bucket of water by the fireplace on Old Christmas Eve, the water would turn to wine at midnight. The stingy old man thought this would be a good way to get some wine and then he could sell it to his neighbors.

"So on Christmas Eve he got a whole heap of piggins and pots and things and filled 'em full of water and set them by the fire a few minutes afore midnight. His old wife was in bed and she heard him yell, 'Hit's turning to wine!' And then right behind him came this voice, 'Yes, and you're mine!' "

Mr. Brown jumped at Peggy when he said that, and she gasped and moved over close to Andy.

"Who was it?" she asked timidly.

"When the stingy old man's wife came to look, the man was gone. And she never knew what got him."

Peggy's eyes grew big. Just then a new and mysterious sound came over the noise of the weather. Plunk! Plunk! Plunk!

"Thunderation, there's another leak!" said Mr. Clark. "Andy, fetch a piggin and set it under that drip."

"Mercy on us," said Mrs. Brown. "It give me a fright starting up like that. I thought something had come to get *me*."

The others laughed except Peggy, whose eyes were growing wider every minute.

"Now, let's quit these scary tales," said Mrs. Clark. "Let's riddle a few riddles. Who'll go first?"

"Me," shouted Dan. "I know one. I know one."

"All right, Dan first."

Dan grinned a gap-toothed grin and said,

"As I went through the garden gap,
Who should I meet but Dick Red Cap.
Stick in his hand, stone in his throat;
If you guess my riddle, I'll give you a groat."

Andy thought hard. He'd heard that one before, but he couldn't for the life of him think what it was.

"A cherry!" Dan burst out, unable to sit quiet any longer.

Andy remembered now when he'd first heard the riddle. He'd heard Isaac tell it last year at the field schoolmaster's.

Kate spoke up next. "Here's a good one," she said.

"I went to the woods and I got it;
I brought it home because I couldn't find
* it;*
The more I looked for it the less I liked it,
And when I found it, I threw it away."

"A huckleberry," guessed Peggy.

"Now why would you think it was a huckleberry, missy?" asked Mr. Clark.

"Well, you go to the woods to get em," answered Peggy. "And sometimes when I look for 'em, I can't find 'em."

They all laughed, and Isaac guessed, "A red bug."

"That's close," Kate answered.

Isaac frowned. "A brier-thorn!" he exclaimed at last.

"That's right," said Kate. "Now it's your turn."

"Wait a minute," Mr. Brown interrupted, going to the door. "Don't I hear something?" He flung the door wide.

"The rain. It's over!" Andy shouted joyfully.

"It sure has stopped," said Mr. Clark. "And looky yonder. Clouds lifting in the west. It'll clear tomorrow sure."

Next morning the sun was shining when Andy went out on the deck. The sky was blue and cloudless, and the air, though still a little chilly, was as sweet and fresh as clover. Andy took a deep breath and went to look over the side. The woods looked so green and bright and new, it seemed a sin and a shame to stay on board that boat.

He wondered what Aswell and Ralph were doing

this morning on the dangerous land route through the mountains. He wished he had his buffalo knife.

On the shore a whole flock of dogwood trees came in sight, covered with white blossoms. In the top of one a red bird sat calling cheerfully to his mate, "What cheer, what cheer, what cheeeeerrr!"

"Ain't that a fair pretty sight?" asked Kate, who had come up beside him.

Andy didn't like to admit it, but it was a fair pretty sight. He watched the dogwoods as far as he could see their gleaming branches. He turned back to the animal pens and let Silas out. The big dog trotted around the deck sniffing the new smells the rain had left.

Finally Silas ran up to help Dan torment the old yellow rooster. Dan poked a stick through the slats of the pen, running it up to the poor creature till it swelled out its feathers in anger and dismay, croaking and pecking at the stick. Silas and Dan both seemed to enjoy this.

Andy climbed on a box and leaned over the side, but his mother called him at once.

"Andrew Clark! Don't you lean over there and fall in. Fetch me a piggin of water. And, Dan, leave that poor rooster be!"

Andy stooped and caught up the wooden bucket

and let it down into the river by the rope tied to the handle. Something made him look up, and he stood open-mouthed as a flock of parakeets went overhead. He had never seen so many of the little green, yellow-headed birds all at one time before.

"Look, Kate, look!" his father cried from the rooftop, and everyone came running to see the little apple-green cloud of birds go winging its way down the river.

"Well, I never!" exclaimed Mrs. Brown, and Andy hauled up the bucket. He set it down with a thump on the deck beside Peggy.

Peggy hadn't been quite sure what everybody was looking at, but now she looked at the bucket. "Andy caught a fish," she exclaimed delightedly.

And sure enough he had. A fish about as long as a finger slid frantically around in the piggin. Now everybody came to look at the fish.

"He ain't very big, son," remarked Mrs. Clark with a smile. "You want to keep him and fatten him up awhile before you eat him?"

"Oh, do keep him, Andy!" Peggy begged.

But suddenly Silas pushed among them and, dropping his head, swallowed half the water in the piggin—and the little fish. Then he looked up in such a puzzled way that one by one they all began to laugh and laugh—even Peggy. It was a wonderful spring morning to be going a long river journey to a new home.

A week later Andy sat on the edge of the rooftop, wondering why he'd ever wanted to go to the French Salt Lick anyway. The river got longer and the flatboat got smaller every day. He was tired of playing games with the others. It seemed as though he didn't have room to stretch out his legs any more. He'd give a barrel of powder for the chance to spend an hour running in the woods.

Suddenly he stood up and glanced about him. Mr. Brown was steering the flatboat to the bank. What was the matter? Why were they stopping here in the middle of the day?

Isaac's head appeared over the roof's edge, and he scrambled up, calling to his father who was steering, "Pa, Pa. Are we going to stop? What for?"

Mr. Brown grinned at his son. "We thought we'd tie up here and let you boys chase rabbits for a spell."

Andy wanted to jump off the boat and swim to shore. He thought he couldn't wait to get his feet on the ground.

A wide meadow stretched away from the riverbank to the foot of a little hill and the grass was so

green and fresh and springy underfoot it was a plea-
sure to run on. Andy's moccasin-clad feet flew over
the field with Isaac close behind, as he headed for
the little creek that flowed into the river.

A few feet from the stream a bird flew up suddenly right under him, and he jumped a yard in the
air, while the bird sailed away screaming, "Killdee,
killdee." Andy flopped backward against Isaac and
the two boys fell in a heap on the grass laughing
and panting. They leaped up and once again ran,
chasing each other, yelling and shrieking, until finally they fell breathless in the grass.

Looking around they could see Kate gathering
wildflowers with the younger children, while Mrs.
Brown and Mrs. Clark spread clothes to dry in the
hot sun. Presently the two fathers walked by carrying
their rifles.

"You boys stay in sight of the boat," said Mr.
Clark. "Remember, now, bears and snakes are hungry and mean this time of year."

"We will," the two boys promised. Together they
watched the hunters go up the hill and disappear
into the woods. They lay on the warm earth watching
the clear blue sky where killdees flapped and
screamed. They broke sweet-gum sticks from a bough
near by and chewed the twigs a bit, and then they
got up and threw rocks at the water striders on the

creek. They jumped back and forth across the little stream while the frightened minnows darted from shadow to shadow.

Now that they were off the boat, they were good companions, though they'd hardly spoken to each other during the past week.

"Come on, Isaac," Andy yelled, coming up to the other boy. "Race you to the top of the hill!"

Andy had to admit that Isaac was a good runner and he had to run hard to keep up with him. But as they scrambled up the slope, pushing their way through blackberry bushes and long grass, Andy's slighter, wirier build stood him in good stead. He reached the top a moment before Isaac, and stood looking around. The blood pumped in his ears and his heart pounded.

As Isaac came up to stand beside him, Andy cocked his head to listen. Ahead and a little to one side, there was a noise of something crashing in the underbrush and a sound of snarling and grunting.

"Animals fighting," Andy said softly. He was about to start off in the direction of the noise when Isaac laid a hand on his arm.

"Your pa said stay in sight of the boat."

Andy twisted his head to look at Isaac. "You scared?"

For a moment Isaac's eyes were angry. "No, I ain't scared. And I reckon your pa'll give you a licking, does he find out."

"He won't find out; it ain't but a little piece over this way," said Andy, trotting off.

Isaac followed through the trees. As they came nearer the noise of fighting they dropped to their knees and crawled through the undergrowth. Andy's heart beat fast with excitement. This was the way his Uncle Aswell hunted in the woods. This was the way a Long Hunter crept up on a buffalo or maybe an Indian camp.

But Isaac glanced behind him. The trees were thick, and he was not quite sure which way they had come. They were out of sight of the boat, and that was certain.

Andy poked his head through an elderberry bush, and stopped. Isaac leaned over his shoulder.

In a clearing just ahead a great elk stood with lowered head, stamping and pawing the earth. A yard or so away a black bear, looking as big as a mountain, reared up on his hind legs. As the boys watched, the bear dropped on all fours and advanced a step, snarling and showing his yellow fangs.

The elk retreated, watching his foe alertly, and the bear reared again. Instantly the elk charged, bellowing with a noise like thunder. Swiftly the bear twisted his huge body to one side, so that the elk missed him, but the big deer swung around at once, thrusting his pronged horns into the bear's haunch. The bear's great paw crashed against the elk's shoulder and a long red wound appeared on the brown hide.

Isaac in his excitement pressed against Andy till the younger boy nearly fell out into the clearing. As Andy struggled for balance, he glanced across the clearing. For a minute he couldn't believe what he saw. It must be a trick of light on the dry leaves, the lean copper-colored face with the tuft of black hair crowned by a feather.

As he stared at the face in the brush, the Indian moved his small black eyes from the two animals and stared full at Isaac and Andrew.

6

Andrew's blood froze in his veins. For a moment he stared into the cruel unwinking eyes of the Chickamauga Indian. He couldn't move a muscle. Then behind him he heard Isaac suck in his breath, and he knew the other boy had seen the Indian, too. The sound seemed to set him in motion and there was a wild scurry of boys, branches and leaves.

Then he was running, back the way they had come, and he could see Isaac a yard or so ahead of him, jumping over sumac and huckleberry bushes as if they weren't there. Andy reckoned he was going pretty fast himself, the trees and bushes were a black blur going by.

Then all at once his foot caught in a brier and he went head over heels among the underbrush. The breath swooshed out of him as he hit the ground and for a little bit he had to lie on the damp earth wondering whether the Indian would scalp him with his tomahawk or take him prisoner.

If I only had my hunting knife, he thought desperately.

Finally he managed to scramble to his knees but his head swam and he couldn't remember which way they had come. He staggered on in what he hoped was the right direction. The undergrowth was thinner now, and he could run more easily as his breath came back to him.

When he heard the Indian coming behind him he really raced. He didn't know he *could* run so fast. His feet never seemed to touch the ground. But he was still scared he had gotten turned around. He ought to be out of the woods by now.

Just then up ahead of him he saw Isaac's fleeing back, and his heart leaped. He wasn't lost, he rejoiced, and at that moment he sped out of the woods and down the little slope. Across the meadow he could see the boat. It looked like half a world away. He was tired and he could hear his own breath coming in great sobbing pants.

And what if they did get away from the Indians and aboard the boat? His father and Mr. Brown were off in the woods and they had the guns with them. Maybe the Indians had already captured the men.

He couldn't hear the Indian behind him any

more. He remembered what his Uncle Az had told him, that any white boy who was a good sprinter could outrun an Indian for a short distance. The Indians did their best running over a long distance. They could run for days without stopping, with the endurance of a horse. Andy had his second wind now and he felt as if he could run a good long way himself.

He raised his eyes to the boat, and suddenly saw Mr. Brown leaning over the side while Mr. Clark swung himself down to the riverbank. Andy's father ran a few steps toward the boys and raised his rifle. Andy was almost even with him when he fired, and the sound of the shot roared in his ears.

He saw Mr. Brown's hands reach down over the side and Andy scrambled up a second after Isaac, and fell to the deck. He lay on the rough floor, wondering if he would ever get his heart to stop pounding and his ribs to stop pumping. He could hear his father and Mr. Brown talking and then Mr. Clark climbed up the side.

The two men pushed the boat away from the shore with the poles, and Andy reckoned he couldn't remember ever being as glad as he was when he felt the river tugging the big flatboat downstream. When the Indians were around, it was a heap safer to be out in the Tennessee River.

Andy sat up. His mother, Mrs. Brown and Kate were peering over the side of the boat. The smaller children sat watching Isaac and Andy. Mr. Clark swung down off the cabin roof, still holding his rifle.

"Where are they, Tom?" asked Mrs. Clark. "I wore my eyes out looking, and I ain't seen a one."

"Wasn't but one after the boys, and he ran back when I fired," he answered, stopping beside his wife. "But we found signs there was a good-sized party of 'em. A hunting party out after meat for the whole village. That's how come us to get right on back. We may have a fight with 'em yet. When you can't see the red devils is the time to worry about 'em most."

He turned and looked down at the two boys. "I reckon you know you like to got yourselves killed, and all of us, too. I told you not to go out of sight of the boat." His voice was stern and Andy quailed.

"You ought to get the licking of your life, but I reckon you got scared bad enough to teach you a lesson you won't forget in a hurry. Next time I tell you to do something, you *do* it, less'n you want your hide taken off."

He gave Andy's shoulder a hard shake.

"Now all of you get back in the cabin. Andy, you knock out the loopholes. If these fellers decide to pick a fight, we'll be ready for 'em."

Andy went soberly into the cabin with the rest. He hoped his pa wouldn't tell Aswell what a wooden-head he'd been. He glanced at Isaac out of the corner of his eye, remembering how Isaac had said not to go, and hoping Isaac didn't remember. Still it *had* been exciting, seeing the fight with the elk and the bear, even being chased by a real Indian. He wished he had had his knife with him. Maybe he could have scalped that old Chickamauga himself.

He began to feel more cheerful as he took the moss and mud out of the loopholes. He held up his hands as though he were holding a rifle, and shot several imaginary Indians, squeezing the trigger as his Uncle Az had taught him, so that he wouldn't flinch and spoil his aim. The Indians would have to be pretty good marksmen to hit a man through one of those small holes, Andy reflected.

He hoped the Indians did come after them. Well, he didn't really hope they did, but if there should be a fight, he reckoned he could do his share. He wished he had his buffalo knife. He glanced out of the peephole he had just cleared, and what he saw made him pause and look more closely.

Andy turned, dashed out of the cabin and climbed up on the roof.

"Now what ails Andy?" asked Mrs. Clark, looking up from her work. "Ain't he done enough running for one day?"

"Look, Pa, quick!" cried Andy on the roof, and his father turned to where Andy pointed.

"Dugouts!" Mr. Clark exclaimed. "Three of 'em!"

"You got sharp eyes, Andy," said Mr. Brown, inspecting the three Indian boats, hollowed-out logs with shaped and pointed ends, drawn up among the bushes along the shore. "I'd have figured them was logs sure."

Andy almost burst with pride.

"Now, son, you get on back down in the cabin. We don't aim to fight less'n we have to, but it looks like we might have to. Tell Mrs. Brown and your ma to get out the bullet mold and lead. And don't get the little ones all riled up. It ain't nothing to worry 'bout."

While Mr. Clark talked, he scanned the shore closely, looking for the Indians. The boat was already rounding a bend, shutting out the view of the dugouts and the shore.

"Now, go on down. Tell your ma I'll be down in a little spell."

Andy scrambled down and burst into the cabin. "Ma! Ma! Pa says get out the mold and the lead. We just passed three dugouts pulled up on the bank. Pa says we're going to have a fight."

"Andy, be quiet. There ain't no call to wake the baby," said Mrs. Clark matter-of-factly. She leaned over the fire and stirred the stew. "Kate, you get the bullet mold. It's in that bundle along with the other cooking pot and the spoons."

Mrs. Brown laid the sleeping Sophronia on a bunk and spread a coverlet over the baby. Now she came to help Mrs. Clark rake up the coals into a pile to melt the lead. Kate rummaged for the mold and Isaac and Andy fetched a bar of lead.

"I wish I had my buffalo knife," mourned Andy.

"Oh, go on!" said Kate tartly. "You couldn't kill a possum with that knife."

"I could, too," Andy retorted. "I ain't scared of Indians."

"Oh, you ain't?" Kate raised her eyebrows. "How come you didn't stop and chat with that one you met back yonder?"

"Now quit that squabbling," said Mrs. Clark sharply.

Andy opened his mouth to say he hadn't been scared of the Indian, when he caught Isaac's eye, and remembered just how scared he had been, so he shut up. He got up and went over to a loophole at the side and looked out.

The riverbank moved by peacefully, the trees in

their new green leaves shining in the sun, and here and there a pink-flowered tree his ma called a Judas tree, or a white dogwood or haw gleamed among the green. But Andy's eyes went to every shadow and thicket, trying to catch a glimpse of bright cloth or feathers, or shining copper skin.

He looked back into the room. Nobody seemed much excited about the Indians. Kate and the two women worked around the fire talking quietly. Peggy and Dan played on the floor with some small gourds, a few mussel shells, and some acorns. Only Isaac had gone to stare out of the loophole at the rear.

As Andy watched, Isaac's back stiffened and he cried, "Yonder they come!"

Andy sprang to the loophole and pushed Isaac aside. For a minute the sun on the water made it hard for him to see, but he soon made out the three swiftly moving dugouts. There were five Indians in each of the boats, but Andy couldn't see how many had rifles. Aswell said that the Chickamaugas mostly hunted with bows and arrows to save powder and lead.

"Reckon Pa's seen 'em?" he asked breathlessly.

"Now what do you reckon your pa's standing up on that roof for?" asked his mother. "Of course he's seen 'em."

Right then the door to the cabin opened and Mr.

Clark came in. "Now don't worry. Just stay inside the cabin." He glanced around to see that all the loopholes were open.

"Pa," begged Andy. "Pa, can I shoot your old musket? Can I? I know where it is."

Mr. Clark gave him a long look. "I reckon you can, Andy. Now don't start shooting first. Let them start anything that's started. And remember that old musket ain't any good for distance. Don't go wasting powder and lead shooting before they come in range. Let 'em come up real close."

His father closed the door and Andrew ran to get the musket. Isaac stood at the loophole, and his mother called, "Isaac, run get a bucket of water 'fore they get here."

Andy took the other boy's place at the rear loophole. He glanced out and saw the three dugouts coming swiftly toward the flatboat. By the time Isaac returned with the water, the Indians were almost up with them. He ran to the side loophole.

One of the dugouts shot ahead of the other two, and those two moved in closer to the flatboat. Andy could see the Indians, bows in hands, outlined against the bright water. His own hands tightened on the old musket. Just a little nearer and he could shoot. Surely they would come close enough for him to shoot.

Suddenly one of the Indians gave a terrible cry, the war whoop, and immediately arrows flew thick at the flatboat. There was a roar of a rifle overhead and then in a second another roar. From one of the boats came an answering fire. One of the Indians must have a gun.

Now surely, thought Andy, wiping his sweaty hand across his shirt, now surely they must be close enough to shoot at. But no, they were going off again out of range, and the two rifles overhead thundered out, one after another. Gradually the two boats moved in closer again. Andrew wondered what had become of the third.

He looked around, but he could see no sign of it, and then he looked back to see the two dugouts closer than ever. Excitedly he sighted along the barrel of the gun. He drew a deep breath, steadied himself as best he could, aimed carefully, and slowly squeezed the trigger.

The noise of the explosion and the jolt of the gun were almost enough to knock Andy flat on his back. He staggered a few steps backward with the wind about knocked out of him and then he pushed close to the loophole, seeking the Indian he had shot at. The man still sat in the dugout, holding his shoulder. Andy was disappointed. He'd aimed for the Indian's head, but the brave's face was twisted in pain and bright blood seeped between his fingers.

Andy stared fascinated as the stream of red increased and ran down the Chickamauga's bare chest and arm. Suddenly Andy flung down the musket and turned away from the loophole. He felt half-sick and the cabin was suffocating him. The room looked so dark and little and the heat from the fire was terrific. Without thinking of his father's warning, he half-stumbled and half-ran to the cabin door and threw it open.

As he stepped out on the sunny deck, a Chickamauga's face appeared over the wall of the prow straight ahead of him. The third dugout had come up under the sloping prow of the flatboat and now the Indians were coming aboard!

"Paaa!" howled Andy. "Oh, Pa."

Then right over his head came the sound of a gun, and the Chickamauga disappeared. Mr. Clark sprang to the deck beside Andy and shoved him roughly to one side, rushing into the cabin.

Andrew cowered against the cabin wall, watching another Indian's hands appear on the top of the wooden fence. His father rushed by him carrying the iron cooking pot. Mr. Clark stepped up on a box and quickly emptied the smoking stew over the occupants of the dugout below.

There were groans and splashes, and Andy ran

back into the cabin. He stood at the door looking out and saw his father jump down from the box and pick up his rifle before he climbed back on the cabin roof. There were a few more shots and then silence for a long while.

Andy went to a loophole and looked out. He couldn't see a sign of the Indians. The river was as lonesome and peaceful as ever. Andy began to recover.

"Come on, Isaac," he said and went out on the walled deck.

Mr. Brown came down from the roof, leaving Mr. Clark to steer the boat. He grinned at the boys. "Here's a couple of real Indian fighters," he said to the women as they came out with the smaller children.

The greatness of the occasion began to dawn on Andy. "I shot an Indian, Isaac," he shouted gleefully. "I did, with Pa's old musket!"

"Kate," teased Mr. Clark, coming to the roof's edge, "how come you didn't take your turn? When your ma was your age, she was a fine shot."

Kate tossed her head. She didn't like her father to tease her about being a tomboy. She tried hard to remember she was almost a grown-up lady, and she liked him to remember it, too.

"Well, what did you do with the stew, that's what I want to know?" asked Mrs. Brown.

"Why, them last two dugouts came in close and tried to keep us a-going at them, whilst the first boat swung around and came up under the front part of our boat where they could climb up. But we out-smarted them and that hot stew did the trick. I reckon a couple of them Indians was ding nigh roasted."

"Well, I don't know what we're going to do for supper," said Mrs. Brown worriedly. "The jerked meat's 'most gone, and the cornmeal's getting low. You didn't get fresh meat this noon, and now the stew's gone."

"Well, I reckon that stew did more good on the outside of the Indians than on the inside of us. We'll get meat afore long," Mr. Brown assured them. "Right now, we got the Suck to worry about. It's getting on for dark and the current's getting faster every minute."

"Yonder comes an Indian village," called Mr. Clark.

"Reckon we'll have another fight?" Isaac asked anxiously.

"I reckon not," Mr. Brown answered. "We're going too fast."

Andy and Isaac stood on a box and watched the village go by. In the dusk, mountains loomed ahead, seeming to block the river. Andy knew that the stretch of river that looped and turned and narrowed to get through these mountains was the dangerous rocky swift-moving section called the "Suck."

He also knew his father dreaded trying to get the boat through such a bad stretch of water in the dark. But they couldn't stop here. On the left bank lay the scattered wooden huts of the Chickamaugas. They were longer and bigger than Andy had thought they would be. One was even two stories high. Now smoke hung like a haze over the huts against the twilight color of the mountains.

The women and children streamed from the huts to the riverbank, where they stood shouting and gesticulating. The flatboat moved swiftly by. Andy saw a tall pole by one of the huts.

"Look, Isaac," he nudged the other boy and pointed. "A scalp pole. Uncle Az said they stretched the scalps on hoops and painted 'em and hung 'em on those poles."

Isaac looked and grimaced. The village was lost from sight. The river went rapidly around a bend, a great loop through the mountains which towered above. It was much narrower and the current was almost twice as fast as it had been. In a minute, they passed another smaller village.

The flatboat went rushing by a big island and immediately beyond that was another town. Andy could hear the roar of the shoals at the beginning of the Suck. The Indians from the last village did not yell, but ran silently along the riverbank through the deepening dusk.

Andy shivered. He was tired and scared. It was dark and the early spring air was chilly now that the sun had gone. The shadowy figures of the Chickamaugas along the bank were mysterious and terrifying.

Suddenly the boat struck something with such force that Andy and Isaac were flung on the deck. The big flatboat bumped and grated over a shelf of underwater rock and then came to a halt. Andy gave a great gasp. They were stuck on the rocks in the Suck, and from the shore, loud above the noise of the river, came the terrible sounds of the war cry!

There was a moment's stillness on board the flatboat. Nobody said anything for a little spell, while from close overhead an owl's cry quivered through the evening air. Then everybody started stirring at once and Sophronia, the baby, began to whimper while her mother crooned to her to be still.

"What happened? What happened?" Mrs. Clark asked, standing in the open door.

Andy moved over nearer his mother and put his arm around Peggy who clung to Mrs. Clark's skirts. His mother's voice was subdued; he could barely hear her above the noise of the shoals, and when Mr. Clark answered, he, too, kept his voice low.

"We're stuck again. We hit a shelf of rock, looks like. Don't be getting riled up. The Indians ain't fixing to come after us in this current, dark as it is."

Mr. Brown scrambled down off the roof and joined them. "Best thing we can do now is have something to eat, then we'll figure out some way to get off here," he said cheerfully.

"That's right," Andrew's pa agreed. "We'll get off here long about moonrise."

"Well," said Mrs. Brown, "I hope it don't take anything tastier than mush to fill you up. Mush is all we have, for a fact."

"Mush is tasty enough for me," Andy spoke up. "I'm near skin and bones, I'm so hungry."

But when he got his trencher of mush and sat down next to Isaac in the dark, with his back to the cabin wall, it seemed like he was so tired and worried he couldn't make his throat swallow, and the mush wasn't good at all.

"I sure wish I had some of that stew," said Isaac after a while.

"I wish I had a big old collop of deer meat," Andy promptly responded.

"My uncle in Salisbury used to have a barrel plumb full of brown sugar, and any time I had a mind to, I could go in and get a lump to suck," Isaac said dreamily.

"Once Pa brought home a gourd full of brown sugar and I had a lump to suck," Andy remembered. He thought about the good sweet taste and the coarse sugar crumbling in his mouth. Maybe Salisbury wasn't such a bad place after all.

Isaac went on. "Lots of times there we had bread made out of real wheaten flour, and my aunt made blackberry and huckleberry pies 'most every day. . . ." He fell silent, dreaming of the riches of Salisbury, and Andy was silent, too.

Isaac was a funny boy. He didn't think nearly so much of shooting Indians as he did of eating brown sugar. Something cold touched Andy's hand, and he jumped like a rabbit. But it was only Silas. Andy fondled the dog's velvety ears, and put his trencher of mush down for Silas to eat.

Kate came over and sat by them, holding Sophronia. Andy drowsed, leaning his head against the wall, listening to the noisy water.

"Come on, boys." Mr. Clark spoke out suddenly in the dark, and Andy jumped to his feet, startled, staring through the blackness. The owl flew overhead again.

Andy climbed up on the roof. On the shore the Indians had built a small/ fire and figures flitted occasionally between the light and the river. Sleepily, Andy took the pole his father handed him. He was so tired he could hardly move his legs.

"Wake up now, son, there's work to do." His father spoke to him sternly, but his hand on Andy's shoulder was kind.

Andy shook his head, trying to rouse himself.

It all seemed like a dream—a bad dream. The roar of the rocks and shoals ahead was putting him to sleep again. He didn't see how he could push the boat off the rocks without falling in the water himself.

"Moon'll be rising in a spell," said Mr. Clark as they stood waiting. "Then it'll be light enough to help us through the Suck. Mostly, we'll have to trust to the good Lord and the high water." He studied the Indians' fire and then turned to his son. "But we can't stay here after the moon's up. The Chickamaugas will be after us before morning if we do."

He shook Andrew slightly by the shoulder. "Do you hear me, Andy? We got to get off the rock!"

They took their places along the roof's edge. Andy stood balancing his pole, drawing in deep breaths of the cold sweet air. The smell of the river and the woods was sharp and refreshing. It made him feel more alert and awake. He leaned on his pole when his father gave the signal and pushed with all his might, but the boat didn't budge. The river rippled by below them. He could see it flash once in a while with the reflection of the Indians' fire.

"We'll move the boxes and lighten this side," his father said. And they all jumped down on the deck.

It seemed to Andy that he must have toted a million bundles before they got things fixed the way Pa wanted them. The next time they pushed, the boat scraped along a yard or so and then stuck again. Mr. Brown wanted to get down in the river and try to see where the boat was caught, but Mr. Clark wouldn't let him.

Andy was waking up now; he didn't feel tired any more. He wanted to get the boat off the rocks and get started. The Indians seemed scarifying in the daytime moving down the river, but here in the black-dark night with the boat stuck, they were enough to make a boy's hair stand straight up on end.

Mr. Brown and Pa got down and moved some more boxes. Andy yawned, stretching his mouth wide and closing his eyes. When he opened his eyes, he thought the end of the world was coming and the sun was plunging across the sky right at him.

"Run!" yelled Isaac. "Get out of the way!"

Andy made a dive for the roof edge and the flaming thing swished by and hissed into the water on the other side.

"Pa!" screamed Andy. "They're shooting fiery arrows at us!"

"I reckon all the folks at the French Salt Lick know it by this time, the way you yell," remarked his father from the deck below. "Looky yonder, moon's rising already. That's how come they could shoot so close to us. But we're a sight nearer the riverbank than I figured us to be."

Mr. Brown came up on the roof and reaching down took some things Mr. Clark handed up, a deer hide and a piggin with a long rope.

"Here, boys, if they try that again, use these," he instructed. "Fill that piggin over the side yonder and be careful the river don't pull you in. Dip the hide in the piggin and wet it good and then beat out the fire with the wet deerskin."

"I know how. Uncle Az showed me how," Andy exclaimed.

"Too bad we didn't all let your Uncle Az show us how to walk to the Lick," said Mr. Brown a little grimly as he left the roof.

Andy and Isaac waited. On a ridge far to the east the distant trees stood out distinctly where the moon's light glowed behind them. In a little, the full moon would ride free of the mountains and its silver light would show the Indians plainly where the boat lay stranded.

Suddenly from the dark shore a spark went up and then another, bursting into fire as they traveled toward the flatboat. Andy waited, breathlessly. He could feel Isaac beside him, tense in all his muscles. Then one of the arrows plopped on the roof right in front of them, and the other fell into the water.

Andy and Isaac dashed at the little heap of flames, swinging the wet deerhide before them. The fire was out in a second and Andy stepped on the last of the sparks. On the deck below, the men had about finished moving the baggage. Mr. Clark was in the front of the boat feeling with a pole, trying to determine how deep the water was ahead of them. Andy could see him very dimly.

Instantly another arrow flamed down through the night and struck at the edge of the roof. The boys ran over with the dripping hide and slung it on the flames. But the arrow had landed in the calking between the logs of the roof, and the dry moss and shavings had caught quickly and were burning brightly almost the whole width of the boat.

"The piggin. Where's the piggin?" Andy gasped.

Leaving Isaac beating at the flames, he ran back to the bucket, but as he reached it, he stumbled on the rough logs. His outstretched hand sent the pail flying and the water spilled uselessly back into the river.

He caught the rope attached to the piggin and lowered the pail into the current. It seemed that it took him forever to bring the bumping, sloshing bucket to the roof. Then he hurried to where Isaac worked away at the fire with the deerhide.

The logs had caught in one or two places now and Andy dashed water on them before he dipped the deerskin in the piggin. The flames were waist-high, and the sweat ran off Andy's face as he worked, slapping and stamping. Isaac worked, too, and he looked up and gave Andy a quick grin. Andy was surprised. Maybe Isaac was going to make a good Indian fighter after all.

Andy grinned back, flapping the deerhide down on the last sparks as Isaac ran across the roof and threw the rest of the water in the piggin on another flaming arrow.

But suddenly something sang by Andy's ear and plunked on the roof logs. He stooped to look. A flint arrow! They'd have to get away from here in a hurry. There wasn't a good deal of choice between being burned and being struck down by an arrow as far as Andy could see. He stood up and two more arrows fell on the roof by his feet.

Andy gave a yell and dropped the deerskin. The moonlight was bright now and he could easily see his way down to the deck below.

"Come on, Isaac," he called. But Isaac stood

calmly, lowering the piggin into the river. "Come on, Isaac," Andy yelled again. "They're a-shooting real arrows. We can't stay up there."

Isaac pulled up the piggin and poured water over the smoldering calking, where a few sparks glowed here and there, before he came down.

"The roof's so wet now, I don't believe they can set it afire," he told his father.

Andy wished he hadn't come down off the roof so fast. He wished he'd been the one to stay up there and pour out the last bucket of water.

"Grab some poles, boys," said Mr. Brown. "We got to be on our way."

Mrs. Clark spoke up from the shadow of the cabin doorway. "Can we get through the Suck in the dark? Aswell said it was such a terrible place."

"We can't stay here," Mr. Clark answered cheerfully. "The water's so high, I believe we can make it with the moon to help out. Come on, boys, push!"

Andy pushed. He pushed until his stomach felt hard and knotted and his ears sang.

The flatboat inched forward. They pushed again. Something seemed to give way, and bang! The current hit the big boat and sent it swiftly down the river. Mr. Brown ran to lower the steering paddle. Mr. Clark turned to the boys.

"Get some sleep, young 'uns. No telling what you'll have to do tomorrow."

Andy went inside the cabin and lay down on a pallet. He was so tired he could hardly move, but he couldn't seem to sleep. His muscles jumped and quivered like a dog's. Every time he'd drop off to sleep, some strange noise would startle him awake. At last, overcome by weariness, he fell into a deep slumber.

When he awoke, sunlight was streaming in the cabin door. Only he and Isaac were still abed. Kate knelt by the fire scouring the breakfast bowls. Breakfast was mush again, but Ma had added some dried apples and a little wild honey to it, and it tasted mighty good to Andy. He and Isaac ate squatting side by side near the hearthstone.

"Where's Pa?" Andy asked Kate.

"Gone hunting."

"Ain't he afeared of Indians?" Andy scraped the last bit of mush from his bowl.

"Pa and Mr. Brown think we're out of Indian country now. We ought to be, we floated the livelong night. I don't know how they stayed awake to steer." Kate looked at her brother and added, "Besides we got to have meat."

When Andrew had finished, Kate handed him

a big bundle of dirty clothes. "Here, tote these out to Ma. She's going to wash clothes this morning. And Pa said tie Silas and Ringo and Gal at the edge of the woods for awhile."

Outside, the two mothers were washing clothes on the bank of a creek which emptied into the river. Dan was wading there below them and Peggy was showing Sophronia how to fish with a stick and no line or hook. Peggy stuck balls of yellow mud on the end of the stick and held the stick in the water. When she drew it out, the mud would be gone, and Sophronia would clap her hands and laugh.

"Let's go fishing," said Isaac. "I crave to sit still awhile."

"Let's scout around a spell first," Andy remarked as he turned and started away from the creek.

"Don't go far, boys," his mother called, and Andy frowned to himself. He wasn't a baby. He could take care of himself in the woods, well as anybody.

But in the cool shade of the trees, he forgot his fretting. A dove cooed in the poplar tree, a woodchuck went shuffling off into the wood. A young deer crashed through the underbrush, stopped when it caught sight of the two boys and turned back.

"I'll go get the old musket," said Andy, starting back, but Isaac grabbed his arm.

"That deer's gone. You'll never see it again. Mine and your pa'll bring back enough meat. Come on."

Andy went with him reluctantly. "Looky yonder, Isaac. There's rattlesnake plantain, good for rattlesnake bites," he exclaimed, pointing to a low-growing plant with prettily marked leaves like the underside of a rattlesnake. "If'n a rattler ever bites you, you chew some of the root of that and you'll be all right."

"I hope I don't never have cause to chew it," Isaac answered fervently.

"And, looky, crinkle-root," Andy went on. "Let's eat some."

He pulled up the little plants, brushed the dirt from the roots and began to eat. For a while the two boys feasted on the crisp white roots.

"I didn't know these were fitten to eat," Isaac said. "You know a heap about the woods and weeds."

He looked at Andy admiringly, and Andy almost burst with pride.

"Az taught me, but I don't anywhere near know what he knows. He knows most everything there is about the woods. What's good to eat and for medicine, and how to make beds and half-face shelters, and how to hunt and trap."

Isaac laughed. "You think a heap of your uncle, don't you? I reckon he must be pretty fine."

"He's the finest man in the whole world and the best Long Hunter there is," answered Andrew positively.

He felt very friendly toward Isaac, and when Isaac took out his knife and began to whittle on a piece of soft wood, Andy didn't say anything about his own long-lost buffalo knife. He just said, "Isaac, you're a pretty good whittler."

He wandered off a little way, leaving Isaac sitting under a tree, but in a second he was back, yelling, "Isaac! Isaac! Come on! Come on!"

Isaac dropped his knife and looked around for Indians. Andy tugged at his shirt sleeve. "Come on, Isaac, help me get 'em."

"What in the nation are we going to get?" asked Isaac, still startled.

"Salad greens! Shawnee salad. We'll carry a mess back to the boat and Ma'll cook 'em for dinner."

When the boys had stuffed their shirts full of the tender green pokeweed leaves, they went back to the boat. "Look, Ma!" exclaimed Andy joyfully.

"Greens!" the women cried, holding up the leaves. "I'm fair starved for something green," said Mrs. Clark. "You boys did a good morning's work. I'd sooner have this than deer meat."

They stood admiring the greens until the sound

of footsteps made them look up. Mr. Clark was approaching, carrying a deer haunch slung over his shoulder. His face was white and lined with weariness, and he moved slowly, limping on one foot.

The others watched him come up. "Where's Pa?" asked Isaac suddenly.

Mr. Clark stopped in surprise. "Ain't he back?" he asked, startled. "He should of been back long ago."

8

"Mr. Brown should have got back quite a spell before me." Mr. Clark swung the meat down off his shoulder and rested it on the ground. "We went along this creek almost a mile east, and then we went about a mile north. We shot a deer, and we each took a quarter to bring back to the boat."

He paused and rubbed his leg. "But my leg was giving out, that place the ball's still in it, and when we started back, I had to give up. The underbrush was so thick and the country so rough, I had to turn back. I came back the way we went, along the creek bank, where it wasn't so overgrown and rocky. But I went slow, I made sure Rob would be here long before me."

Mr. Clark rubbed his cheek and looked worried. "Maybe he went after another deer or turkey or something. Or maybe he couldn't get through and had to turn back, too."

"Do you think . . . do you think Indians got him?" asked Isaac, glancing at his mother.

Mr. Clark frowned. "I don't reckon so. We didn't see a sign of Indians in the woods. We've come a good way past the last Chickamauga town. I reckon he'll come in after a while. I'm going to bed. I've got to get some rest afore my leg gives out complete." He stopped and added, "But if Rob ain't back in two hours, you all wake me up and I'll go after him."

Mr. Clark climbed wearily aboard the flatboat. Andy and Isaac got the deer meat into the cabin. The two women set about cutting it up for cooking and drying. Mrs. Brown looked anxious and Mrs. Clark was reassuring her. The boys went out on deck.

"Andy," said Isaac, "where's that old musket of your pa's?"

"In the corner by the fire. Why?"

"I aim to get it," answered Isaac slowly. "I aim to get it and go after my pa."

Andy stood still with his mouth open. He had felt sorry for Isaac when Mr. Clark had come back without Mr. Brown. He had wondered what in the nation a boy did without his pa. Isaac had seemed quiet and grown-up, telling his mother not to worry and going about matter-of-factly, as if he expected his pa back any minute.

Andy would never have thought he'd want to do a thing like this. He stared a minute at Isaac and then he said, "I'll get the musket, Isaac. I'll go with you. And we'll take Silas and go find your pa!"

Andy sneaked the musket out of the cabin; the two boys climbed down from the boat and untied Silas. They couldn't decide whether to follow the creek or not, but when Silas bounded off into the woods away from the creek, the boys followed.

"We'll have to go sort of northeast," said Andy.

"Well, that way's east and that's north, so we must be going northeast now," said Isaac. "Do you reckon we ought to yell for Pa?"

"No," answered Andy. "If there was Indians about, they'd hear us sure. We got to keep walking and look for signs."

"What kind of signs?"

"Arrows and campfires," replied Andy. "Places where the bushes are broke down, where maybe your pa put up a big fight. Or maybe blood."

Isaac stopped and gave Andy a long look. "I don't think Indians got my pa," he spoke. "I think he got lost or maybe hurt some way. If'n Chicka-maugas got my pa, we might as well go back now. What in the tarnation could two young 'uns like you and me do?"

Andy scratched his head. "Well, not much, I reckon. I didn't mean it about the Indians, Isaac."

They went on through the woods, moving soundlessly on the deep moss. The trees were so thick that almost no sunlight lit the way for them. Even Isaac began to go more cautiously and look nervously around him. Andy wished it was Aswell with him instead of Isaac.

Finally Isaac stopped and said uneasily, "Maybe we ought to fire that musket. Then if my pa's around he'll hear it and fire his rifle."

Andy started to say something about Indians, but then he paused and replied, "All right."

"Is it loaded?" asked Isaac.

"No," answered Andy. "After I shot that Indian I cleaned it and put it away."

"Well, where's the powder and lead?" asked Isaac.

Andy stared at him.

"Where's the powder and lead, I said?" Isaac asked again.

Andy swallowed. "I . . . I didn't bring none," he stammered at last. "I plumb forgot, when I was sneaking out the musket."

Isaac looked all around him. "Can you find your way back here from the boat? You go get the powder, and I'll stay here."

"I reckon I can get back, but how come you ain't coming with me?"

"I aim to stay here, in case my pa should come back this way. And I don't want Ma to see me, else she might put me to work. I'm going to find my pa if'n I have to stay out here a week."

"Then I'll leave you the musket," said Andy.

"And what could I do with it with no powder or bullets?" asked Isaac angrily.

"Well, Silas can stay with you then," said Andy hastily, and turned back the way they had come.

Isaac held Silas by the back of the neck till Andrew was out of sight, in case Silas should get any notions about following his master. The boy and the dog settled down under a tree to wait. Isaac was glad Silas was with him. Silas would warn him if bears or Indians were about. But surely Indians hadn't got his pa.

Silas got up and began to wander about. Isaac wondered whether his father had had to turn back and go around by the creek as Mr. Clark had done. He wished Andy would hurry back. Perhaps he ought to have gone back with him and hid at the edge of the woods. Perhaps he ought to get up and go meet Andy.

No, he'd come this far, he wouldn't turn back. Suddenly Silas began to bark and howl from a patch of sumac bushes to one side. Isaac sprang up in fear and bewilderment.

Indians! he thought in panic, but before he could make his feet move to start running, he had had time to realize that it wasn't Indians Silas was barking at. The dog was making such a noise as Isaac had seldom heard. He crept up on the noise and peered over the bushes.

Silas was leaping frantically at something on the ground, howling and leaping away, barking and whining. At first all Isaac could see on the ground was a dead rabbit. What had got into Silas?

Then he saw the snake coiled a foot away from the rabbit, its mouth opened, its tail raised and the rattled tip going back and forth so fast that it was just a blur. Silas must have tried to take the rattlesnake's dinner away from it. The snake was a big one, and it was a terrifying sight coiled there with its white fangs gleaming.

Isaac looked about for something to hit it with. He picked up a stick, but it did not look big enough. He reached for another, and at that moment the snake struck Silas in the shoulder. The dog leaped in the air, snarling and yelping, and the snake fell back on the ground.

Isaac snatched up a stone and rushed at the rattler, heedless of his own danger. The stone struck the snake squarely, crushing its head, and Isaac turned to look for Silas. He began to run, looking for signs that the dog had come this way.

He had to find Silas. He didn't know what he would do when he found him, but he couldn't let Andy's dog die out here in the weeds. He'd let him get snake-bit, and now he had to find him.

Isaac sped through the shadowy woods. "Silas! Here, boy!" he shouted.

Something in the bushes grunted and crashed off. Isaac glanced over his shoulder.

"Here, boy!" he shouted again.

Was that a dog's bark ahead? He ran faster. The way was downhill now, and the woods were dry and rocky. The trees thinned, and the undergrowth was hard to get through. Blackberry runners tore at his legs and tripped his feet.

"Silas!" he said, panting.

Suddenly to one side he heard a shrill call. He dropped to the ground. Indians! Indians had got his pa and come after him. And he had killed Andy's dog that might have warned him, and he was too tired to run another step.

Andy ran beneath the great branches of the tulip trees and oaks, coming out under the dancing leaves of the sycamores that grew along the riverbank. He hid the musket under a bush and moved toward the flatboat. He eased himself up the side and peered over.

Nobody was in sight except Dan and Peggy, who were eating cold ash cake near the cabin door. And, praise be, his father had left his powder horn and his pouch slung down on a box right there not two feet from Andy's hand.

He slipped down on the deck and stuffed the pouch and the horn inside his shirt. He was already wriggling over the side again when Dan began to wail, "Andy, take me with you."

Kate flew out of the cabin with the ax in her hand. "Andrew Clark, where've you been? Go get us some kindling. Now hurry. Here we got a good dry back log and not one thing to light it with. And the meat going to waste!"

Kate all but pushed him over the side. Andy ran and hid the powder and lead with the musket before he went after the kindling wood. He got a good big pile of firewood while he was at it. It didn't take too long and he was afraid Kate might get to pestering him about what else he had to do, if he looked like he was in a big hurry and only brought in a little dab.

He thought about Isaac out in the woods. Of course, Isaac wasn't really alone, he had Silas with him. All the same, Andy knew it took a lot of courage for Isaac to stay there in the woods, alone and without a rifle or even a hunting knife. That little old pocketknife would be no help, of course. It was all right for carving your initials on trees or school benches, but no good in the woods.

He stacked up the wood by the hearth, slipped out the cabin door, over the side of the boat, and into the woods. He picked up the musket and the ammunition and started off to find Isaac.

As he went along he watched for signs to show where the two boys had been before. Here they had broken through the huckleberry bushes, there they had snapped a twig.

He went along, "trailing" himself, as Aswell had showed him. In a little hollow where the moss was damp, he could see the prints of moccasins and he tried to figure out which were his and which were Isaac's.

Going on, he saw a single pine all by itself in the midst of a group of oaks, a landmark he had noticed before. And there was the big hickory tree with the lightning sear down one side. It wasn't but a piece now. Silas ought to come running to meet him.

He walked on, swinging the musket and wishing he had his hunting knife. He'd be a real Long Hunter then. He was glad he had the musket anyway. It was kind of dim and lonesome in the woods. He wondered why Silas hadn't heard him.

He stopped, looking around. Had he missed the way somewhere? Surely this was the place where he'd left Isaac. He turned and looked back, but the forest behind him looked all the same, dark and still.

He went on a ways and came to a place where a big dogwood tree spread out its branches and white blossoms, and the moss beneath it was spattered with creamy petals. He turned back, going north a bit more, and came out on the edge of a creek with a kingfisher's hole gaping from the other side.

Andy stood a minute, gazing at the hole, and watched the kingfisher fly out and up the creek with a loud rattling call. He turned and began to run. He ran back to the hickory tree with the lightning scar and then retraced his steps to the spot where he was sure he'd left Isaac.

He searched in a circle around that spot until he was sure he had made no mistake. He knew this was the place where he'd left Isaac less than an hour ago. And now Isaac and Silas were gone!

9

Isaac lay in the tall grass as still as a stone. But by and by the sound came again and this time it didn't sound like Indians. It sounded like a cry for help.

Isaac jumped to his feet. "Pa!" he shouted. "Pa, I'm coming! Pa!"

"Here! This way, over here!" came his father's voice.

Isaac ran forward, but his father shouted again, "Watch out, don't come too near!"

Isaac didn't know what he was supposed to watch out for, but he slowed down, and by and by he saw. A great hole yawned in the hillside. It looked as though the earth had given way and sunk into the ground.

"Pa!" Isaac gasped. "Are you in there? Be you hurt?"

"No, I ain't hurt. But you be careful. I don't aim

to have both of us down here. Come up real slow and be sure the earth holds."

Isaac crept slowly to the edge and peered over. There was his pa, covered with mud, staring up from the bottom of a pit about fifteen feet deep. The bottom of the pit was soft mud and pools of black water, but the sides were smooth as glass.

"Go fetch some vines, son. Enough for me and this deer meat, too."

Isaac ran. He followed his father's instructions and pretty soon Mr. Brown stood on the solid ground, having pulled himself out by the vines Isaac had woven together and tied to a tree. Then he pulled up the deer haunch.

"Now, how'd you get out here?" he asked, and Isaac told him.

"Well, Isaac, I'd have thought you had better sense than to come traipsing out in the woods like this. A hothead like Andy, now, he might do such a fool thing, but not you."

Isaac stared at the ground. "I reckon it was foolish," he answered finally. "It just seemed like a boy ten years old ought to go after his pa when he got lost. I shouldn't have let Andy come. And oh, Pa, what am I going to do about Silas?"

Mr. Brown looked serious. "I don't know. We'd

best get on back to the boat now."

Suddenly Isaac pointed. "What's that?" he asked.

"It might be Silas," Mr. Brown answered. "Come on. Don't walk up on him too sudden. He might start running again."

When they came up to him, Silas lay in the grass, moaning and whining. He looked up at Isaac and wagged his tail feebly. His shoulder was swollen and knotted. Mr. Brown stooped by him.

"He ain't too bad off. You said the rattlesnake'd just killed a rabbit. It wouldn't have much poison left. Silas didn't get much. He'll be all right in a week or so."

Isaac picked the big dog up and started after his father. His arms ached and sweat ran down his face. He couldn't see where he was going and he stumbled on every root and rock he came to. But he knew Andy had left Silas in his charge, and Andy would never forgive him if the dog died. So now the least he could do was carry Silas back to the boat.

Andy was back by the creek when he first heard voices. He clutched the musket. There wasn't a place to hide. What little underbrush there was under those great trees was so low and scrubby a possum couldn't hide in it.

Would he have time to climb a tree?

He looked around desperately at the huge trees. A boy with his hands full of musket didn't stand much chance of getting up one of those big trunks. He slid behind a tulip tree, pressing himself against it. If it was Indians, surely they wouldn't expect to find a lone white boy out here in the woods.

Then he heard Isaac's voice, clear and plain. "It was right here, Pa. Yonder's the rattler. He's a big 'un, ain't he?"

Andy bounded from behind the tree and raced toward the voices.

"Isaac! Isaac!" he called.

"Over here," Mr. Brown answered.

Andy saw Isaac carrying Silas first, and his heart stopped. He should have known better than to leave Silas with Isaac. Now Isaac had let Andy's dog get killed by a rattlesnake. That was just like a town boy, not to watch after somebody else's dog.

He ran up. "What's the matter with him?" he asked angrily.

Isaac laid the dog on the ground.

"He's been snake-bit," said Mr. Brown. "But he ain't real bad off. The rattler'd just killed a rabbit, so he didn't have much poison for Silas."

Mr. Brown turned and pointed. "Yonder's the snake."

Andy's eyes widened. "He's a big feller. Who killed him?"

Isaac told what had happened, and Andy stood silent in admiration. Isaac might not be a woodsman, but it wasn't because he was scared. It was a fine brave thing, to kill a big snake like that, and then to go chasing through the woods after Silas, without a gun, and maybe Indians or bears waiting behind every tree.

And all for Andy's dog!

Then Mr. Brown told how he was coming up the hill with the deer meat when all of a sudden the earth gave way beneath his feet and he fell into a deep mud pit. There was so much water in the bottom, he figured it must have been an underground stream that dug out the hole, leaving just a thin layer of earth on top so that the least little weight would cave it in, though there was no sign of the pit beneath.

There hadn't been any way to get out, and he had just had to sit and wait till Silas had come howling by, and then Isaac, and Mr. Brown had hollered.

"I was mighty glad to see Isaac," Mr. Brown said gravely. "But let me tell you boys something. You might of got killed, tearing around in the woods this way. It was a tomfool thing to do, and I mean to give Isaac a licking when we get back to the boat."

The boys hung their heads, but inside Andy couldn't help feeling that they'd behaved pretty well in the woods. Maybe they shouldn't have gone, but they'd found Mr. Brown and hadn't got lost or done anything Aswell wouldn't have approved of. Except coming away without the powder and lead. And anybody might do that the first time they went out with a gun.

Isaac cut off the snake's rattlers and gave them to Andy. Andy picked up Silas and they started back to the boat.

Andy and Isaac got a whipping for going in the woods after Mr. Brown. It wasn't much of a whipping, and when Mr. Brown told Mr. Clark and the womenfolks what the boys had done, he made it sound so brave and exciting, Andy hardly noticed the stinging on his legs any more.

The flatboat stayed tied up until mid-afternoon while the menfolks slept. Mrs. Clark made cold and hot compresses for Silas' shoulder and Andy tried to make him drink a tea made of colic root, but the dog wouldn't touch it. The sun blazed down and Andy rigged up a deerskin to make a shade on the deck for Silas.

Andy's mother, Mrs. Brown and Kate sat on the deck piecing a quilt. The children played on the shore and Isaac and Andy untied the other dogs, Gal and Ringo, and let them run for a bit. They practiced throwing rocks at a target and Andy beat Isaac.

When the men got up, they untied the boat and went floating down the river once more. For dinner they had the Shawnee salad cooked with bear's grease, and some of the venison and ash cake. It tasted so good, Andy couldn't get enough.

Andy and Isaac stretched out on the warm rooftop after supper, as the boat floated through the golden spring twilight, listening to the men talk. They were talking about Muscle Shoals.

"I heard tell in low water you can cross the river without getting your feet wet, there's so many rocks," said Mr. Brown.

"And the river's so wide there, even high water like this don't make it much better," added Mr. Clark. "But Aswell says a heap of flatboats went through it with Colonel Donelson. We'll just have to trust in the Lord."

"Yonder's the first star," said Isaac, pointing. "Wonder are there any Indians up there?"

"Wherever there's people there's Indians to fight 'em, I reckon," said Mr. Brown wearily.

"Once I heard the schoolmaster in Salisbury say people that lived on the stars didn't have no heads and their eyes was in the middle of their chests," said Isaac.

"Well, he shouldn't have said such a thing," answered Mr. Brown. "It's against the word of God. The Bible says the Lord put people on the earth, not on the stars."

"Once I heard a man named Alexander Bibb say a body that knew the signs could read his fate in the stars. He was staying the night at my house, on his way to New Orleans. If he hadn't been my guest I would have told him he was as full of lies as a sieve is holes. Why, according to him, I could go out and look up at the stars and tell how much corn my bottom land would bring next year."

"Well, look up there now, and see will we get over Muscle Shoals," said Mr. Brown.

"I can't tell, but I don't need the stars to tell me it's time to tie up and get some sleep," said Mr. Clark, yawning. And Andy agreed.

The following day they floated down the river almost all day. The sun shone hot and bright, and Andy nursed Silas under the deerskin tent. The dog lay with his eyes closed, groaning softly once in a while, but toward evening he roused himself a little and drank a great quantity of water.

"There!" exclaimed Mrs. Clark triumphantly. "He's mending already. I never seed a dog that was dying drink water."

Andy felt better at once. Shortly after that they heard the familiar roar of shoals, only louder and higher in pitch than they'd ever heard it before. It was a worrisome noise, like a mosquito singing, Andy thought. They tied up where they were and everybody went to bed early.

Tomorrow they would have to go through Muscle Shoals, the longest and most dangerous stretch of shoals in the river.

The next morning they were up hours before the sun. Andy, Isaac, and the two men worked hard rearranging the boxes and bundles so that the flatboat would be properly balanced and the baggage secure and steady. When it was done, they went to eat.

"Everybody eat hearty," said Mr. Clark. "We'll be busy all day; we may not eat again before night."

Andy sopped his ash cake in the good stew and ate hearty. He wished he had some buttermilk. He did miss buttermilk.

"Come on," called Mr. Brown. "We'll go untie the boat and in a spell we'll see the shoals."

Everybody went out on the deck except Mrs.

Clark, who sat by the hearth dipping the wooden trenchers in a pot of hot water. Andy looked back at her and hesitated. He badly wanted to see the Shoals but he wanted to ask his mother something, too. With a reluctant glance outside, he moved back to the hearth.

His mother looked up and smiled. "Be you still hungry?"

"No'm," Andy answered, watching her rub the bowls. "No'm."

He was silent a minute, and then he burst out, "Ma, what's the matter with Isaac? He wants to go to Salisbury and be a merchant. I figured he was scared to be a woodsman, but he ain't. He went after his pa, and he went after Silas and he wasn't scared. But how come does he want to be a merchant?"

His mother sat back and stared at Andy. "Well, for mercy's sake, Andrew! What give you the notion everybody in creation had to be a Long Hunter? Just because your Uncle Aswell never sleeps under a roof or eats anything but bear toes don't mean the rest of us has to. Why do you think we're going to the French Salt Lick?"

Andy shook his head.

"You think we're going to spend the rest of our

days living in a cabin? No, we're going so we can have houses and farms and churches, maybe someday a settlement there as big as Salisbury. And the settlements that grow the quickest are the ones where the most merchants live and bring the most things for people to own."

Mrs. Clark smiled at Andy again.

"In this country a merchant has to work as hard and be as brave as anybody else. And remember— the best reason for Long Hunters like you and your Uncle Az is to find good places for settlements for the merchants. Now git!" she said, "or you'll miss seeing the Shoals."

Andy ran out on the deck, feeling happier than he had in a long while. He just hadn't thought things out before. He reckoned it did take Long Hunters and merchants both to make a world. And a Long Hunter could be friends with a merchant, especially if the merchant had showed how brave he was by rescuing the Long Hunter's dog.

"Isaac!" he shouted, scrambling up on the roof. "Can you see it yet, Isaac?"

As a matter of fact, they didn't come on the Shoals all at once. The river got wider and wider and shallower and shallower. Finally the banks were so far off you could hardly see them, and the surface of the water looked choppy and different from the smooth river they had left behind.

Rocks and small islands stuck up here and there, and then became more and more frequent until it seemed the boat couldn't squeeze between any two. Mr. Brown stood at the steering paddle, while Mr. Clark stood on a box at the prow to try to pick out the deepest channel and help Mr. Brown miss the rocks.

Andy guessed it was the rocks and islands that made the boat seem to skim along so fast. They sped by before Andy could get a good look at them.

"Looky, Isaac," said Andy, pointing to where the foaming water fell over a little falls a foot or so high, and stretching twenty feet across the riverbed.

"I hope we don't have to go over nothing like that," Isaac answered.

"Me, too," remarked Andy.

Just then the flatboat scraped shudderingly against a rock, swung to one side, and bumped across a rock shelf. The huge logs of which it was built groaned and creaked, and Andy cast an anxious look down at the deck.

Would the big boat hold together?

Suppose it had been damaged or weakened back there at the Suck when they were stuck? Suppose it should go to pieces here in the middle of this boiling water? Andy wondered if Isaac was as scared as he was.

Mr. Clark turned and motioned for the two boys to come down to the lower deck, where it was safer.

Isaac went below first and sat down on a box. Andy sat beside him. How the boat flew along, swinging back and forth among the rocks, scraping and bumping. Under his feet Andy could feel the logs sliding against each other as the boat twisted in the currents, and it made his hair stand on end.

He thought about the miles and miles of shoals still ahead of them and he shivered a little. Maybe he ought to go sit inside the cabin with the women and children. No, it would be worse not to be able to see what was going on. It was just that he hadn't expected to go so fast.

Andy jumped upon a box and looked over the side. The rocks and islands were thicker than ever. He could see the tumbling foaming water stretching ahead for miles. The water rushed along over rapids and cascaded down from ledges of rock like a furious animal.

The boat shot ahead as light as a chip of wood. It made Andy's heart jump into his mouth as the flatboat dropped down, down, down and then plunged into the boiling water that waited below.

All of a sudden Mr. Clark began to yell and wave his hands and point. Isaac jumped up beside Andy to see what was ahead.

The river was different. Andy couldn't see what it was, but it looked like a long waterfall. He looked quickly up at Mr. Brown, struggling to turn the great boat. And when he turned back to look at the river again, he saw that there really was a waterfall in front of them, a high one that stretched all the way across the river.

Andy couldn't see what they were going to do. If they went over that fall, the flatboat would surely break all to pieces. But they'd have to go over it. There wasn't any other way.

Isaac gripped the top of the railing hard with both hands. His eyes were wide in his pale face. But he turned and grinned at Andy. Andy was glad he hadn't gone in the cabin. If a boy who was going to be a merchant could stay and face the danger, so could a boy who was going to be a Long Hunter. So the two friends stood side by side.

Now Andy saw why Mr. Brown was trying to turn the boat. There was a narrow gap in the ledge where the water poured through without falling—a gap not much wider than the boat itself. It looked as though they'd never make it, for the boat was being swept nearer the falls every minute.

The flatboat jolted over a hidden rock and Andy fell off his box. He was just as glad. He didn't want to see what happened when they went over the falls. The roar of the water got louder and louder till it was almost deafening. The big boat bumped and rocked and seemed to tilt to one side and hang suspended in the air a moment; then it shot ahead and once more began its twisting turning voyage down the shoals.

Andy climbed hastily onto his box again and looked back at the falls. He shook his head unbelievingly. How they got through that gap he'd never know. But now that it was safely past, the falls didn't look to be more than four feet high. A few minutes ago, he remembered, it had looked fully fifty feet high.

He'd never forget this, he reckoned, if he lived to be a hundred years old. Why, Aswell hadn't even been over Muscle Shoals falls. Wait till he told him how scarifying it was.

Later they all agreed it was a miracle they had got through the gap, even though the boat had gone through slightly askew. After the falls nothing else seemed quite so bad though there was a long, wearying, frightening way to go, more crosscurrents and rapids, rocks and shoals. Mr. Clark and Mr. Brown changed places several times.

At noon the men figured they had reached the end of the shoals, and they tied up for a few hours' rest. And then a wonderful thing happened.

Silas got up and limped over and ate the bowl of mush Andy had set out for him. Andy was so happy he nearly cried.

10

They got to the French Salt Lick exactly one month and nineteen days after they had set out.

From Muscle Shoals on the trip seemed pretty dull to Andy. There were no more shoals or rapids. Twice they saw Indians, hunting parties who stood on the riverbank and silently watched the flatboat sail by.

Once an old she bear with two cubs chased Mr. Brown to the boat when his rifle failed to fire. Game was pretty scarce. Mr. Clark said it was because of the hard winter three years before, when many animals died of freezing and starvation.

Andy remembered that winter well. At first he had thought all that snow and ice was fun, but then after a few weeks it seemed as if he was cold all the time. They couldn't keep the cabin warm no matter how they tried, and going out in the wind was like stepping out into ice water, no matter how many clothes a boy had on.

And food was scarce—he was hungry all that winter and spring, clear up till the first potatoes were dug. That was the winter when Colonel John Donelson had set out with his great company of flatboats to come to the French Salt Lick. Andy was glad they hadn't gone with the Colonel.

Several times Andy and Isaac went hunting with Silas and one of the men. They learned a lot about hunting and once Andy shot a deer. He did not kill it, but Mr. Brown killed it a few minutes later, and Andy was very proud of himself. After that he tried to teach Isaac about hunting, but Isaac only grinned at him and said he'd rather learn about hunting from Silas.

And sure enough in a few days Isaac killed a rabbit all by himself. He ate it all by himself, too, and tanned the skin to make Sophronia a bonnet.

Some days they fished over the sides of the boat. They caught a few catfish, enough for supper once in a while, and it was a change from game.

But Andy lay awake nights sometimes, dreaming of roast'n'ears and snap beans and potatoes, buttermilk, and butter. He was hungry all the time, just like that winter three years ago, and out in the woods he spent more time hunting something to eat than he did something to shoot.

"Isaac?" he asked one day, as the two boys sat on the cabin roof.

"What?" answered Isaac.

"Does your uncle at Salisbury have a cow?"

"He's got three," replied Isaac. "And he's got four horses and a flock of hens and two sheep."

"What's he need three cows for?" asked Andy.

"He don't *need* 'em, he just *has* 'em," Isaac explained.

"Oh," said Andy, and then a little shyly, "Do you still want to go back to Salisbury?"

Isaac thought a minute. "No," he said slowly, "I reckon not. I've come all this long ways and we've been through so many troubles, seems like I couldn't stop now and go back. And when we get there, I figure there'll be plenty of work to do. And a place you've worked so hard for, you might as well stay there and see that work don't go to waste."

They laughed together. Andy was glad. Now Isaac was his very best friend, and he didn't want to think Isaac might go off and leave him. He hoped they'd always be friends.

One day they saw a great herd of buffalo. In a savannah the big brown beasts grazed by the thousands. Isaac and Andy and Kate, who had never seen buffalo, hung over the sides and watched the herd as long as they could see.

"Thousands of 'em, just like Aswell said," Andy murmured, awestruck.

"They're so big," exclaimed Kate.

"They must be blind, never a one of 'em looked up when we went by," remarked Isaac.

"They can't see good," Andy answered. "If the wind had been right, they'd have smelled us quick enough."

A day or so later they came out into the Ohio River. Andy hadn't known a river could be so big. He gazed across the wide stretch of muddy water in wonder. They tied up for a day and a night. Mr. Brown and Mr. Clark tore down the cabin on the flatboat and took off the wooden wall that surrounded the deck, lightening the load as much as they could. From now on they must pole against the current rather than float with it.

The nights were warm; no one minded sleeping in the open. But they were all nervous about Indians. They kept the dogs loose all the time to give a warning.

Then they started on the hard journey up the Ohio. The men poled, Andy and Isaac took turns steering, and the others walked.

It was a long dangerous weary time. Andy didn't

see how they expected to make the journey up the Cumberland River after they left the Ohio. His own legs ached from standing, the sun beat on his head all day long, and he did not see how his father and Mr. Brown stood the hard work they did all the long hours of the day, pushing and pushing the big raft—for that was all that was left of the flatboat—against the current.

At last one day they came to a place where a small river flowed into the Ohio.

"Is it the Cumberland?" they asked themselves, but Andy thought not, it was hardly bigger than a creek.

"I don't know," replied Mr. Clark wearily, shaking his head. "It seems like it ought to be, but I don't know."

"Any which way," Mr. Brown said, "let's tie up here at the mouth for the rest of the day."

Mr. Clark gazed up the little river. "I never figured it would be so hard to get here. I shouldn't have let Ralph go with Aswell. He should have come with us to help pole. I just don't think the two of us can get this boat up the river to the Lick."

Andy looked away. He couldn't bear to see his father so tired and beaten. Silas went sniffing off into the woods and Andy went after him. He didn't want to stay with the grown-ups if he could help it.

Suddenly Silas gave a little yelp and went sniffing off another way, and then he began to run.

Now what's he after? Andy asked himself. He stood waiting a minute, undecided whether it was safe to go with Silas or not. *If only I had my buffalo knife,* he thought miserably, *I wouldn't be scared to go anywhere.*

But Silas had stopped and was looking back, waiting for Andy to catch up with him. And he was *grinning.* There was no mistaking the delighted look on his face.

"Well, thunderation!" Andy exclaimed aloud, and followed Silas.

And then Silas began to yelp and bark and out of the bushes stepped a tall figure, a man with a brown beard who said, "Down, Silas, down, boy!" and turned to meet the boy who, half-laughing and half-crying, came flying toward him.

"Oh, Az! Oh! Aswell!" shouted Andy.

"Where in the nation have you folks been?" asked Aswell. "Ralph and me been waiting for you three days. We 'bout figured the Chickamaugas had you. Where's your pa?"

"Uncle Az!" shouted Andy again. "I been over Muscle Shoals. We went over a waterfall must of been forty feet high right spang dab in the middle of the river. I killed a deer, leastways I shot him.

And I shot an Indian. We fit the Chickamaugas, Az, just about a hundred of 'em and Pa poured stew on 'em, and that's how come Silas got snake-bit, on account of the meat. . . ."

"On account of what meat?" asked Aswell. "Slow down, young 'un. I got time to hear it all. And I want to see your pa. Where's everybody got to?"

"Pa, oh, Pa!" Andy yelled, dashing ahead. "Ma, it's Az! Everybody come quick!"

Andy almost fell in the river.

In a minute they were all crowding around Aswell and everybody was talking at once. The dogs barked and the chickens cackled and Andy shouted until Aswell began to laugh.

Then in a minute they were all laughing, all the weariness and despair fallen from them now that Aswell was here. When finally they quieted down, Aswell explained that he and Ralph were camped a little way up the river.

They had come a few days before to wait for the flatboat, since they knew that getting the big flatboat up the Cumberland River would be almost too much for the two men. And Aswell had brought a horse! With a horse to do most of the pulling and the four men to do the poling, they'd be at the Lick in no time.

"Well, we've got to hurry," said Aswell, his face

a little grim. "There ain't any Indians about now, but there's sure to be plenty in a few weeks. As soon as they can get in a supply of meat to leave in the villages, they'll be after us like bees after honey."

Aswell went to get Ralph and the horse, and the rest of the afternoon was spent telling the two newcomers all the adventures of the river travelers.

"Well, thunderation!" said Aswell. "Ralph and me come over the mountains and we never saw an Indian. We didn't see an Indian or a bear or a catamount. We never even had a hard rain. The only trouble we had the whole way was one time when one of the cows started swimming downstream and we couldn't get her to go back."

He laughed and Ralph frowned. "That danged cow! I reckon I chased her five miles up and down that river."

"I shot an Indian, Az," Andy spoke up.

"And four bears and twenty deer and eight buffalo and Dragging Canoe himself, I reckon," said Aswell, rumpling Andy's hair. "You'll make a Long Hunter yet."

The next day they set out for the Lick. Andy and Isaac had to steer again, but it didn't seem like work now. And they had another job, too—leading the horse on the riverbank. At night when they tied up, the boys played over the baggage, piled in the center of the raft. They joked and laughed with Ralph and Aswell.

Andy's ma told him he was the biggest nuisance she'd ever had to put up with. But she didn't mean it. And it wasn't until the third day, when Andy lay on his pallet trying to sleep, that he thought of something.

How was he going to tell Aswell that he'd lost the knife, his beautiful buffalo-bone knife? He couldn't do it, he just couldn't. After that, though he seemed as lighthearted as ever, a dozen times a day he stopped to mourn for his wonderful knife and to ponder how he would ever be able to tell Az.

Time went by and then one morning Aswell and Ralph said they were within a day's journey of the Lick. By evening they would reach the fort.

The long journey was safely over at last. They started out happily, even Andy. But as the day wore on, he felt less and less happy. Clouds came drifting across the sky and piled up thicker and thicker until the day was as gloomy as Andy felt.

Somehow he knew that he would *have* to tell Aswell about the knife before they reached the Lick. With only a mile or so left to go, Aswell got off the boat and waded to the shore where Andy was leading the horse along the bank.

Andy didn't say anything when Aswell took the bridle from his hand, but after a little he said, "Uncle Az, do you like Isaac?"

"Yes, I do. Isaac's a good steady boy with sense enough to get on in the world."

"He wants to be a merchant when he grows up," said Andy dolefully.

"Good," remarked Aswell. "You'll need merchants at French Salt Lick."

There was another long silence, and then they rounded a bend and straight ahead of them on top of a bluff was a big fort.

"Home," said Aswell, and Andy looked at the stern log fortress sitting on top of the rocky cliff. A path wound through the dark cedar trees to the cleared space around the fort.

Home? To Andy it looked cold and forbidding and hateful. He wondered what in the world they had come all this way for, to end up in this desolate place.

Aswell said, "It's a funny thing. You remember that knife I gave you before we left? Well, when Ralph and me set out the next morning, I found a knife just exactly like it in one of my bags! Now what do you think of that? I've a mind to give it to Isaac. A good boy like that needs a knife."

He slid his hand into his shirt and drew out—Andy's buffalo-bone knife! Andy stared at it a moment.

"Az," he stammered. "It's my knife. I dropped it that night when I went to sleep setting on your truck. *Don't* give it to Isaac. I'll take good care of it, I promise."

Aswell threw back his head and laughed. They reached the foot of the bluffs directly under the stockade. Aswell unhitched the horse and called to Isaac.

"Tie her up, Isaac. Here we are."

The men on the flatboat stopped poling and stared upward. Isaac waded to the bank and began to tie the flatboat to a tree.

Just then the clouds parted, a big patch of blue showed through, and the gold light of the setting sun fell over the western hills. It shone on Aswell's tan face and his brown beard, and it bathed the log fort in a light that made it seem a kinder, happier place.

"You know," Aswell said, turning to Andy, "it's a good thing you didn't have that knife with you on the river."

He placed the knife in Andy's hand.

"If you'd had it along, there wouldn't be a bear or a deer left up and down the Tennessee River.

Now how soon do you want to go buffalo hunting and what will you do with the first one you kill?"

"I'll eat it," replied Andy.

"But what'll you do with the hide?" teased Aswell.

There was a sound of footsteps and Isaac came up to them.

Andy stood in the last rays of the sunset, looking from his knife to his uncle and then to his best friend.

"The hide?" he said, grinning. "I know what I'll do with it. I'll trade it to the merchant!"

WILLIAM O. STEELE (1917–1979) was born in Franklin, Tennessee. It was there, as a boy exploring the fields and woods around his home, that he developed an interest in the history and pioneers of Tennessee. Later, as a grown man, he would write his historical adventure stories from his home on Signal Mountain, where he could look out at the same hills his characters saw during the days of the early frontier. William O. Steele published thirty-nine books over his long career, many of them award winners, including *The Perilous Road*, which was named a Newbery Honor Book in 1959.